"Make me feel strong again . . ."

Mark's eyes closed slowly as his lips descended upon hers. Merry drank of his kiss as he did of hers, and she felt her soul opening to him like a thirsty bud unfolding to the rain. Simple, unmitigated joy filled her, a growing peace that had the power to overcome any obstacle. Nothing could harm her, nothing could frighten her, nothing was too much for her, as long as Mark was by her side.

His hands moved beneath her sweater, pushing it upward; then he covered the expanse of abdomen with light nibbling kisses. Her skin tingling from the touch of his lips, Merry murmured, "Mark, there's just one thing . . . ."

"Anything, for you, love. . . ."

EASY ACCESS
REBECCA FLANDERS

Harlequin Books

TORONTO • NEW YORK • LONDON
AMSTERDAM • PARIS • SYDNEY • HAMBURG
STOCKHOLM • ATHENS • TOKYO • MILAN

ABOUT THE AUTHOR

A native of Georgia, Rebecca Flanders began
her writing career at the age of nine. She
completed her first novel by the time she was
nineteen and sold her first book in 1979.
Rebecca enjoys painting in oils and watercolors,
as well as listening to and composing music.

Harlequin Intrigue edition published March 1985

ISBN 0-373-22013-8

Chapter One

The man who ambled out of the weathered, peeling shack that served as a gas station and general store was whippet-thin and dour-faced, dressed in an oil-stained gray shirt and cotton pants. He circled Meredith Griffin's dusty orange Vega once, suspiciously, before coming to stop at her window. "What'll it be?" he demanded flatly.

Meredith let out an impatient breath that was only partially mixed with uneasiness. She had been driving all day and was in no mood for this. Her nerves were tightly strung, and the five-minute wait in front of the sagging gas pump had not improved her disposition any. The man had seen her drive up, and so had his two cronies—the ones who still leaned against either side of the door of the building, drinking beer from the bottle and shooting undisguised glances of hostile curiosity her way. It had taken three blasts of her horn to get any attention at all, and now Meredith wished she had just driven away. Twilight was falling, and she did not like the dark, unfriendly figures of the two in the doorway. The sharp face of the man at her window was no more reassuring. And the isolation of the place was unsettling.

"Fill it up," she snapped, nervousness making her tone shorter than she had meant it to be. "With regular."

The attendant wandered off toward the rear of the car.

Meredith sighed and leaned her head back against the seat. What a godforsaken little place it was. When Roger had said remote, that was exactly what he meant, but somehow Meredith had not been expecting anything quite this bad.

She was not certain what exactly she had been expecting. Should the truth be told, she had gone into this adventure with the same spirit with which she met every other challenge of her life: impulsively, thoughtlessly, expecting nothing and open for anything. Roger had tried to dissuade her, and failing that, had attempted to prepare her, but most of his lectures had fallen on deaf ears. Meredith had only to look at the bleakness and agony in her parents' faces to know that it was not thought that was called for but action. And this was one action that was long overdue.

Out of the corner of her eye Meredith saw one of the shadows at the door straighten and move toward her; her muscles tensed automatically. But the specterlike figure only walked a few steps to deposit his beer bottle in the oil barrel that served as a trash can. The clatter of glass against metal split the evening stillness and made Meredith grit her teeth. The man walked back to his position beside the door, and it must have been only

Meredith's imagination that told her he had never once taken his eyes off her.

Well, she rationalized, *it's a small town. Off the beaten path. They probably don't get too many cars through here with out-of-state plates, and naturally they're curious. They don't mean to be rude; it's just their way.*

Making herself relax, Meredith straightened up and even smiled a little in their direction. The two men stood there, watching her, as implacable as gargoyles in the fading light.

"Oregon, huh?"

The flat, dry twang in her ear made Meredith jump, and she turned to meet the face of the service-station attendant at her window. His expression did not make it clear whether he had a personal grudge against Oregon as a state or whether it was merely people who came from Oregon he despised. Meredith decided to ignore it. She had been driving too long, that was all. She was tired and hungry and tense, and her imagination was running away with her. These people really weren't hostile toward her. The two men in the shadows really weren't sinister. And she was usually much more sensible than this.

"That's right," she returned pleasantly, but she found herself wondering why it was taking so long to fill her gas tank. She wished the man would move away from her window.

"What're you doing down here?" he demanded bluntly, and that was definitely not the tone generally associated with a friendly resident welcoming a stranger to his hometown.

For a moment Meredith hesitated. But she was going to be here for a while, and perhaps the only way to break the ice with these people was to make the first overture herself. Besides, she did need directions, and that was what gas stations were for, wasn't it?

"Actually," she explained pleasantly, "there's a man here I was hoping to meet. Reverend Abraham Samuels? I believe he's with an organization called the Source of Enlightenment. Perhaps you could—"

But almost before the words were out, she saw the harsh shield come down over the man's eyes; in the middle of her sentence he turned and walked away.

Meredith twisted around in her seat to follow his retreat, and what began as gaping astonishment swiftly changed to a scowl. That was more than rude. It was explicit.

The gas pump clicked off; a moment later the attendant appeared at her window again. "Twelve fifty," he said shortly.

A lack of tenacity had never been one of Meredith's shortcomings, but she knew how to quit when she was ahead. There was no point in beating her head against a brick wall with this fellow, either for the sake of friendliness or information. She could get directions and information in town, and this little hole-in-the-wall service station was beginning to get on her nerves. She whipped out her credit card and thrust it toward the man without smiling.

He took the card and studied it for a long time

in the dim light. "Don't take it," he pronounced at last, and returned it to her.

Meredith glared at him for a moment before turning to search through her purse for some cash.

"You planning on being around long?"

Meredith did not answer. She did not want to wait for change and was relieved when she came up with a ten, two ones and two quarters. She folded up the money and presented it with a flourish.

The attendant took his time about accepting her payment. He stared at her coldly, expressionlessly, and his eyes reminded Meredith of a snake. Then his grimy hand closed around the cash. "Won't find no place to stay around here," he said, and it sounded like a grim promise.

For a moment Meredith stared openmouthed after the figure as it sauntered away, wanting to say something witty and sarcastic or even to demand an explanation. But the two figures at the building seemed suddenly taller and the twilight abruptly more menacing. She swore to herself softly and realized she was in no mood to deal with the eccentricities of small-town hicks that night; antagonizing the residents would not make her stay there any more pleasant.

Meredith turned the key and jerked the car into gear. For the first time in the probable history of the automobile, the little Vega left black streaks on the asphalt as it screeched away.

THE EVENTS that led to Meredith Griffin's pilgrimage to Stonington, Kansas, had begun three weeks earlier with a phone call from the family attorney, Roger Blake. After six months of trying, he had finally been granted an interview with Merry's brother Kevin. Only the interview had never taken place. Kevin refused to see him, or so Roger was told.

In actuality, the story really began over a year before, when Kevin left home. Or perhaps it went back even further than that, to his childhood, his infancy, to those important formative years or the turbulence of adolescence when someone, somehow, had done something wrong, had failed Kevin in some way.

Meredith scowled at herself and rubbed the back of her neck irritably, further disarranging the stiff braid that had bound her honey-blond hair through an already rigorous day. How many times had she lectured her parents on the uselessness of blaming themselves for Kevin's personal weakness, and here she was doing the very same thing herself. For a moment she felt a brief surge of anger toward the brother she had loved and protected for all of her twenty-eight years. Did he have any idea what he had done to their lives? Did he even care?

She slowed the car to swerve around a man-eating pothole in the middle of the road and noted with relief the blinking neon lights of what appeared to be a motel just up ahead. Roger had not stayed overnight, so he could give her no forewarning about what kind of acommodations she could expect in this place, but at this point it did not matter. A bath and a bed were all she needed, and the next day she would begin the business of her mission refreshed.

The motel was a long, squat concrete building circa 1920, and the sign announced Four-Star Motel. "Sure," Meredith muttered to herself dryly, but she felt a little better as she swung into the parking lot. Rest was all she needed now.

There were only three or four cars in the lot besides hers, and red neon bulbs on the office window spelled out Vacancy, leaving the No above it unlit. "So, big surprise," Meredith again commented to herself as she got out of the car and surveyed the slightly less than four-star accommodations around her. She doubted the place was exactly turning away customers in droves.

She paused for a moment, placing her hands in the small of her back and grimacing a little as she stretched away the taut muscles of a day's confinement. The light spilling through the open blinds of the motel office window was bright and welcoming, and it was easy to put the day's rigors behind her now that she was out of that car. She could even laugh a little at herself for letting the scene at the service station get to her. A couple of weird old codgers, a ramshackle building and a hassle over a credit card and she was ready to turn the experience into an Alfred Hitchcock thriller. "You're going to have to do better than that, Merry old girl," she told herself dryly, reaching inside the car for her purse and the leather duffel bag, "if you're going to start running all over the country acting like some modern-day Nancy Drew."

She smothered a grin as she swung the strap of the duffel bag over her shoulder and strode toward the registration office. Talking to herself was a habit Meredith had picked up when the car radio had broken down midway between Idaho and Wyoming. She knew it was one she was going to have to break, and quickly, if she expected to maintain any credibility at all with the esteemed Reverend Samuels.

The door sported a collection of credit-card symbols, an announcement that welcomed traveler's checks, and to Meredith's very great relief, a sign pointing to an in-house coffee shop. Food. A bath. Rest. It sounded like heaven.

The interior of the office was small, but not as bad as she had expected. The tile was grayish-white, but more worn than dirty, the walls a nauseating color of green, but they looked freshly painted. The woman behind the desk was rounded and plain, with frumpy brown curls and too much makeup. She gave Meredith a curious but not unfriendly look as she came in.

"Hi." Meredith set her bag on the floor in front of the desk. Her good humor was so greatly restored by her journey's end that she found the smile coming naturally to her lips. "I need a single room with a double bed—king-sized, if you have it." Meredith was a tall woman and used to sleeping spread-eagled on the bed. The shortage of king-sized beds was one reason she hated traveling.

The woman reached down and retrieved a registration slip from under the desk. "Double is all we've got," she pronounced. "One night?"

"Maybe longer." Depending on whether or not, Meredith thought, she could find a motel with a king-sized bed. She did not know how long she would have to be here, but she was far too self-indulgent to spend one unnecessary moment in less than total comfort.

Meredith filled out the registration slip quickly and passed it, along with her credit card, across the desk. She had not until that moment realized how peculiarly the woman had been watching her. She felt a sinking feeling in her stomach now as she saw the implacable eyes lower deliberately to the registration slip and study it a long time without touching it. *Good Lord,* thought Meredith in mounting frustration. *What now?*

There was no sound but the buzz of fluorescent lights and the softness of Meredith's own breath in her ears until the schoolroom-type clock overhead clicked once, loudly, and the minute hand moved a notch. The woman placed one finger on the credit card, as though she found the touch of it distasteful and pushed it back across the desk toward Meredith. Her thin scarlet-painted lips drew even tighter, and one corner turned upward with something very close to a grimace of disgust.

Meredith stared at her in astonishment. "What is it with you people and credit cards, anyway?" she demanded. "Your sign said—" She broke off impatiently and took out her wallet. She was too tired to fight about it that night. "All right,

I'll pay in traveler's checks." She paused in the act of drawing out the check folder and inquired with forced politeness, "You *do* take traveler's checks?"

The woman took her registration slip and very deliberately crumpled it into a ball. There was no mistaking the antagonism in her eyes; it was so close to hatred that it took Meredith's breath away. "We're full," she said.

For a moment Meredith couldn't speak. She simply stared at the woman, her eyes round, her lips parted with an incredulous breath. When she found her voice, the first words that came to mind were a rather dim protest. "But your sign said—"

"Bulb's burned out," returned the woman shortly, and the contemptuous expression in her eyes professed no shame for the lie.

Meredith stared at her. The parking lot was not even half full. The bulb was not burned out. The woman had been perfectly willing to register her until she saw her name. Meredith had not felt so stunned, so confused and helpless, since she was in the third grade and her teacher had slapped her palm with a ruler for a crime Meredith had not committed. And she simply did not know what to say.

But then, just as it had with that long-ago teacher, a sense of righteous indignation began to surface, anger mingled with her own innate pride and stubbornness, and Merry felt temper tingle in her cheeks. "Now you wait just a minute—"

"I said we're full," the woman interrupted harshly, her voice rising a note. The other woman's eyes swept Meredith's figure once, filled with challenge and tinged with spite. Merry could not help being shaken by the ugly curl of the woman's lips, the hardening of her eyes. The roll of her voice was low and threatening, and when she leaned forward on the desk, a gust of sick-sweet perfume wafted Meredith's way; she took an automatic step backward. "We got no use for your kind around here," she hissed. "You gonna get out of here, or do I have to call the sheriff?"

Meredith Griffin was not used to being discriminated against. She was not used to dealing with hostility. Everyone liked her. She was welcome anywhere. No one had ever threatened her in her life. And the first incredulous words that came to her lips were "What do you mean—*my kind*?"

The woman sniffed and straightened up, her eyes very cold. "Just exactly what I said."

"Now you listen to me." A slow rage was pulsing through Meredith's veins and stiffening every muscle of her body. She did not understand this; she couldn't believe it. But she knew when her rights had been violated. She had simply never had to fight for them before. Her face was taut with controlled anger, and her eyes narrowed, but she had to clench her fists to stop the trembling. "There are laws against this kind of thing. I have money, I have credit, and you can't refuse—"

The woman turned and deliberately walked away. The small door that led to a room behind the desk closed, and Meredith was left alone, impotent with her rage.

Several incredible scenarios flashed through

Merry's mind. She thought about banging on the little desk bell and threatening at the top of her lungs everything from a lawsuit to a government investigation. She thought about helping herself to one of the keys just to teach the old bag a lesson about lawful discrimination. She thought about calling the police herself.

And in the end she was left still standing there alone, helpless, angry and more confused than she had ever been in her life.

Meredith was not going to make a scene. What good would it do? She was not going to stay where she wasn't welcome, and she could hardly force the woman to be hospitable. With a soft, vicious oath, she slung her bag over her shoulder. Just what the hell was she supposed to do now?

She turned to march out of the building, and the window caught her reflection—a long-legged woman in stovepipe tan corduroys and short matching jacket, a rumpled blond braid, a strong square face. There was nothing unusual or offensive about the way she looked. What did she mean, Meredith thought with a new surge of indignation, by *your kind*?

Meredith let the door clatter loudly behind her, and it wasn't until she had started the engine of her car and sat there with no place to go that she made the connection. The man at the gas station said she wouldn't find anyplace to stay around there. He had looked at her credit card. The woman at the desk had been perfectly willing to register her until she looked at the credit card— and saw Meredith's name.

"Damn!" It was a soft exclamation, filled with more wonder than anger and hiding an uneasy chill that crept without warning down Merry's spine. What had the man done, then? Called the woman at the motel and told her to be on the lookout for one Meredith Griffin and to refuse her accommodations at any cost? Did these people have some kind of underground network to protect them against strangers? And why?

It was incredible. Meredith shook her head a little, as though to dismiss the entire night with its farcical undertones of conspiracy and espionage from her mind. Roger would never believe this. It was just too much like a made-for-TV movie. What did these people have against her?

She might have exaggerated that episode at the service station, but the hostility she had confronted inside that motel office was unmistakable. The woman had refused her service. Meredith still couldn't believe that. What had she done to deserve such treatment?

There was probably a very good explanation, she decided as she pulled her car back onto the highway with no particular destination in mind. Maybe the owner of the service station and the owner of the motel were related. Maybe they just didn't like strangers coming into their town. And that was ridiculous, of course. Both of them would have to make their living off strangers coming through town. No, it was that they didn't like *her*. Meredith didn't understand it. Not at all.

It was too dark to read the map, and Merry had no idea how long she would have to drive before she reached the next town. Again she swore, loudly and colorfully, to herself all alone in the car. She didn't need this; she was in no mood for this. And how dare they? How dare that woman turn her away? Anger started to boil again, and her strongest inclination was to turn the car right around, and storm back into the motel office, if for nothing else than the satisfaction of giving the woman a piece of her mind. . . .

Meredith's headlights flashed on a neat white sign that said, "Welcome to Stonington. Population—"

Merry missed the population because she saw just up ahead the startling signs of civilization— low sand-colored buildings intermixed with stately whitewashed structures, streetlights, spotlighted sign that said, "Stonington Hotel—Vacancy."

Meredith braked sharply and made a short right-hand turn underneath the sign. Her lips were compressed grimly and her neck tight with stubbornness as she jerked on the emergency brake and got out of the car. She would be humiliated once, twice at the outside, but if these people intended to give her trouble over a room, they had damn well be prepared for a fight. She would drag the magistrate out of bed if she had to. She would call the mayor. She would have papers served against them that very night if they so much as looked as though they didn't want to accommodate her there.

The lobby of the Stonington Hotel was quite different from the Four-Star, but Meredith paid scant attention to the details as she strode toward the desk. She got a brief impression of roominess, of light beige carpets and comfortable-looking imitation-leather chairs drawn up in sitting groups, and of the soft sounds and smells of a restaurant opening off the main foyer. She was so angry, and so determined, she wasn't even hungry anymore.

The young man at the desk looked up with a pleasant smile as she approached. "My name is Meredith Griffin, and I want a room," she announced, deciding to get all the preliminaries out of the way and face the worst first. Just let him try. Just let that sappy-faced kid even try to kick her out this time.

But the boy showed no reaction other than a slight puzzlement at her belligerent attitude. His smile never wavered as he placed a registration slip on the desk. "Single or double?" he inquired pleasantly.

Meredith was slightly taken aback but answered cautiously, "Single room, double bed...king-sized if you have it."

"We have several nice rooms with king-sized beds," he replied and turned to check the board of keys. "Yes, room 204 is available." He placed the key on the desk with a smile. "You'll like it; it has a nice view of the park. Will it be just yourself, Ms Griffin?"

Meredith paused on the third line of the registration slip, glancing back up at him skeptically. But there was nothing on his face but well-trained friendliness, and she began to feel slightly foolish. "Yes," she replied. "Just me."

"Will you be staying with us long?"

"I'm—not sure." Meredith completed the registration slip and handed it to him.

"If you have a credit card," he suggested, "we can imprint it now and save you some time when you check out."

Now Meredith definitely felt foolish. She handed him her credit card meekly.

The Stonington Hotel could not have been friendlier. The young man told her that her room was all ready, explained to her about the restaurant and the swimming pool, which would open in two weeks, offered to send someone for her bags and wished her a very pleasant stay. Meredith declined the offer of help with her bags and walked in something of a daze to her room, where she found the lights were already on and the thermostat set; even her bed was turned down.

"Talk about your fast service," she murmured to herself, and set her bag down in the middle of the floor.

The room was not a luxury suite, but it was as attractive and modern as anything a thriving motel chain would have to offer. The decor was peach and green. There was a writing desk, a long bureau, a roomy closet. Two comfortable chairs were drawn up before a round table at the window. The bathroom had a separate dressing area. And the bed was, indeed, king-sized.

"Well, well, well." Meredith tested the firmness of the mattress and the crispness of the sheets with her hand, then wandered over to the heavy print draperies and pulled them back a fraction, but she could see nothing but darkness outside. She trailed her hand over the polished veneer of the dresser. "Nice."

Obviously, she had jumped to a mistaken conclusion about the town. Two unfriendly greetings, probably purely coincidental, and she was ready to accuse them all of foul dealings. She had to grin at her own foolishness and shrugged away the humiliating scene in the motel office. *Paranoia,* Roger would have said. *The social disease of the cocaine age.*

Who could guess what that other motel clerk's problem was. Maybe she didn't like Meredith's accent or the way she dressed. Maybe she disapproved of a womann traveling alone. There were people like that in the world, Meredith supposed philosophically. She had gotten off to a bad start, but it was behind her now and she was not ging to let one—no, two—distasteful incidents distract her from the real purpose of her trip.

Meredith sat down at the desk and picked up the telephone. She did not have to wait for an outside line, and she dialed her parents' number direct. They had asked her to call as soon as she arrived.

There was even stationery on the desk, Meredith noted absently as she listened to the ringing on the other end of the line, and a pen. Both displayed the name of the hotel in gold letters and, in the same gold, a peculiar little logo that was an ellipse with two intersecting V's in the middle. She picked up the pen and absently began to trace the logo on a sheet of the stationery, but when the telephone had rung ten times, she decided her parents were obviously out. Good for them. They deserved some relaxation every once in a while.

She hung up the phone and debated for a moment over calling Roger. Roger had been her family's lifeline in the past months, and he had been more than a little concerned about her making the trip alone. She could at least call him and tell him she had arrived safely.

But that was one duty Meredith did not need much of an excuse to evade. Roger was caring, involved and diligent. Meredith did not know what her family would have done without him over the past six months. He deserved all their gratitude and all their consideration. Roger was wonderful, but he was also Meredith's boss. And he was trying very hard to fall in love with her, which was the major reason Meredith had refused to allow him to accompany her on the trip.

She thought the phone call to Roger could wait. Right now she was travel-worn and hungry, and all she wanted was a quick bath and a change of clothes, then a hot meal in the restaurant downstairs.

Chapter Two

It was Friday night, and the hotel restaurant was apparently the only place in town one could go for an evening out. Meredith made that observation as she stood at the roped entrance to the dining room and was told by the pretty young hostess that there would be a thirty-minute wait. Meredith sighed and relayed the message to her rumbling stomach, and the hostess suggested, "There's room in the lounge if you'd like to wait. I'll call you when your table is ready."

Meredith considered her options. It was possible she could find a fast-food restaurant if she drove far enough, but the very thought of getting back into the car made her queasy. Possibly there was a café or diner or even a drugstore open somewhere along the main street, but exploring the streets of a strange town after dark was not high on Merry's list of fun things to do. And if there was any other decent place to eat around there, the hotel dining room would undoubtedly have been far less crowded. A nice strong drink was just what she needed right now, Merry decided, and allowed the young woman to direct her to the lounge.

The lounge was a small area that was screened from the restaurant by potted plants and elevated tables. Softly lit but not dim, it was an attractive atmosphere in dark woods and imitation leather. The crowd in both the lounge area and the restaurant were well dressed and nicely mannered, and, it seemed to Meredith on first glance, mostly young.

Meredith had never been the kind of woman who stopped traffic or solicited wolf whistles as she walked down the street, but for the second time that day she found herself wondering what it was about the way she looked that attracted so much attention. Basically, she had always considered herself a fairly plain-looking woman. She was tall and large-boned, with an athletic build, broad shoulders and few curves. Her hair, thick, coarse and honey blond, was her most distinguishing feature, but even it was not shown off to its full advantage. It was cut bluntly to the middle of her shoulder blades and parted in the middle across a broad forehead in a style that made her face look even more militant than it already was. Her skin tone was uneven and needed skillfully applied makeup to conceal its most obvious flaws; her eyes were hazel and not large enough to be striking. Her lashes and eyebrows were that sandy color that afflicts most blondes and had to be darkened with makeup before they were noticeable at all. The Roman nose, wide mouth and aggressive chin all combined to form a face that was, on first glance, quite ordinary and not particularly attractive. Then why was everyone staring at her?

There was none of the hostility in the atmosphere that the encounter with the testy service-station attendant and the antagonistic motel manager had put Meredith on guard against, but nonetheless she thought she detected some curiosity in the glances she received as she hesitated at the entrance, looking for a place to sit. It was nothing specific, nothing she could pinpoint, but she felt as though she were drawing attention to herself, and she self-consciously ran her finger around the waistline of her high-buttoned slacks, making sure her blouse was tucked in. She even glanced surreptitiously at her shoes to make sure they matched—it wouldn't be the first time she had started out the door in her house slippers, for Meredith tended to be absentminded when she was upset. But no, her shoes were conservatively dressy patent leathers with two-inch heels and ankle straps, and they were both black. *Imagination,* she scolded herself, and started toward the bar where there were two or three widely scattered empty stools. *Paranoia again*.

Meredith slid onto a barstool and casually fingered the bodice of her blouse, checking for missing buttons. This was ridiculous. It wasn't the first time she had gone out alone or the first time she had sat at a bar by herself. What was it about the place that made her feel she had just walked into a formal gathering in her underwear? She just couldn't shake that feeling that people were staring at her. Not suspiciously or hostilely but merely curiously, with perhaps a slight undertone of disapproval, the way a congregation might look at a woman who walked into Sunday morning services in a swimsuit.

And that was when Meredith realized why she felt so out of place. None of the other women were wearing slacks. There was an even mixture of men and women in the lounge, and most of the tables in the restaurant were occupied by couples; a few of them over forty but for the most part young, all-American-looking, clean-cut young people. The men were dressed in sports jackets or conservative shirts with ties, and the women—every single one of them—were wearing skirts and blouses or slightly dressy street frocks.

Merry relaxed on the stool and let out a breath of amusement and amazement, relieved that it was something so simple. Only a woman's sixth sense could turn the feeling of being inappropriately dressed into a telegraph of danger. It still made her slightly uncomfortable, but at least this time she knew it was her imagination taking over, and she assured herself she really wasn't fashion-conscious enough to let it bother her.

The bartender did not look old enough to even be drinking, much less serving drinks, but his cheerful, fresh-washed countenance was a welcome sight to Meredith. He didn't seem to mind that she was the only woman in the room wearing slacks. "What can I get for you, ma'am?" he asked.

Meredith smothered a smile at the unaccustomed sensation of being called "ma'am" in a bar, and she answered, "A Bloody Mary, please, no ice."

The bartender's smooth young face was suddenly shadowed with disturbance, and again Meredith was amused. He had never heard of a Bloody Mary? They *were* hiring them young here. "Vodka and tomato juice," she explained, but there was an uncomfortable expression on his face as he looked at her.

"I'm sorry, ma'am," he explained, keeping his voice low, almost as though he were afraid of embarrassing her. "We don't serve alcohol here."

Meredith's eyes flew wide in astonishment. "What do you mean you don't serve alcohol. This *is* a bar, isn't it?"

A slight flush tinged the bartender's cheeks. "No, ma'am," he answered. "That is, it's a lounge, but we don't serve intoxicants."

Intoxicants. Meredith stared at him. He said the word as though it left a poisonous taste in his mouth, and his expression was reminiscent of one he might have worn had she suddenly offered him a twenty-dollar bill and the key to her room. She opened her mouth to ask another question, but he interrupted quickly. "We do have a nice selection of soft drinks, though, and fruit juices—almost anything you want."

"Except vodka," murmured Meredith dryly, and his face fell again. He looked so disappointed and chagrined that it was hard not to smile, and Meredith said, "Tomato juice, then—with lots of ice."

The young man looked vastly relieved as he turned away.

"Curiouser and curiouser," Meredith murmured absently, watching him cross busily to the other side of the bar, and a male voice very close to her ear startled her.

"Welcome to Wonderland, Alice," it said, and Meredith turned her head to meet a pair of vastly amused gray eyes.

It was bound to happen sooner or later. She had been caught talking to herself. A prickling sensation heated her cheeks, and she tried to dismiss it with a small nervous laugh. "Or the Twilight Zone, whichever the case may be."

The man's eyes sparked with appreciation for her quick recovery, and that should have put Merry at ease. For some reason it only made her feel more nervous.

Meredith did not know why she hadn't noticed him when she first sat down, but then she had been too involved with her own state of attire to notice much of anything. Perhaps on first glance there would have been nothing to distinguish him from the crowd, but that was on first glance. When Meredith looked at him now, she knew there was nothing ordinary about this man at all. Not at all.

He looked as though he belonged on the cover of a Regency novel. Slim, broad-shouldered, beautifully built, he exuded the grace and savoir faire of born nobility. Aristocratic nose, artfully shaped chin, beautifully sculpted lips. His thick dark hair swept over his forehead from a side part and curled up a little over his collar. She could easily imagine it pulled back at the nape and tied with a black ribbon, his shirtfront heavy with ruffles and his narrow waist banded by a satin cutaway coat. There was a faint line near the left corner of his mouth that suggested his lips were accustomed to twisting into a swift, cynical smile, but right now the curve of his lips was pleasant and open and hardly even noticeable as a smile.

He was sitting casually with one arm resting on the bar, his hand cupped around what Meredith could only presume to be a glass of orange juice, and that delicate slim-fingered hand should have been emphasized with a gracious fall of lace from the wrist. Debonair, she thought. Elegant. Rakish. A little ruthless beneath that finely carved, polished silk exterior. He brought to mind visions of highwaymen and refined drawing rooms and innocent maidens ready to be seduced. And like any good rake, he had a perpetual gleam of mocking self-knowledge in his eyes. No, there was definitely nothing ordinary about the man.

This unexpected leftover from a more dashing, romantic era was dressed in a narrow-wale teal-blue corduroy suit and a conservative pale blue shirt with a small maroon stripe, buttoned at the collar. He was clean-shaven and well-groomed—Meredith realized she had not seen a beard or a moustache in the entire hotel—and he couldn't have been much over thirty. He looked friendly and at ease, yet he carried with him an aura of lazy self-confidence and alert awareness that could be most unsettling. Everything about him proclaimed on an almost subliminal level that despite his efforts to blend into the crowd, he was not really a part of the place. Meredith suspected he would stand apart from the rest wherever he went.

The corduroy suit had a designer touch; it was not bought off the rack. The oxford shirt had French cuffs. The longish cut of his hair was a definite contrast to the almost military length that seemed to be preferred by the rest of the male patrons there. He wore a gold Seiko watch, and his cologne, which had a mellow scent, was not something that could be purchased in a department store. Although little things, they were big-city touches that seemed slightly incongruent with the isolated small-town atmosphere.

It had not taken Meredith very long to make those assessments—a matter of seconds, really—but he had picked up on her scrutiny immediately. It registered in the slight deepening of the laugh lines around his eyes and, yes, the curve of his lips into the hint of a Byronic smile. Otherwise, there was no suggestion of anything whatsoever out of the ordinary as he explained easily, gesturing toward the bartender, "It's a dry county."

Meredith lifted a skeptical eye brow. "Then why did they open a bar in the hotel?"

He laughed softly. It was a sound that put Meredith immediately at ease. "I suspect the hotel was here before the county went dry, so the new management just tried to make the best of it. It's still the only place you can get a decent meal for thirty-five miles."

"Do you live around here?" Meredith inquired, and then she could have bitten her tongue. What was she doing making conversation with a stranger at a bar—and in a strange town, no less? He would think she was trying to pick him up. She knew better than that. She had had enough problems that day. The last thing she needed was to get tangled up in a pair of dancing gray eyes.

And once again it annoyed her that those eyes seemed to register her embarrassment and be amused by it. But he only answsered easily, "Mmm-hmm. I have a condo a few miles out of town, actually. What about you?"

Again Meredith could not prevent an astonished lift of her eyebrows. "Condo? I didn't think that this town was big enough for anything like that." Roger certainly hadn't given her that impression. But then Roger hadn't been here very long.

"We've made a few improvements the last few years," he admitted. "The town is growing fast. Ah, here's your drink."

Meredith gave the bartender a smile of thanks that she hoped disguised her distate for the glass of flat red liquid before her. But before she could even bring herself to taste it, the man beside her took her glass. She protested, "What are you—"

He gave her a conspiratorial "shhh" and brought the glass down below the shelter of the bar. In a moment he returned it to her, eyes twinkling. "Taste it," he invited.

Meredith gave him a skeptical look and ac-

cepted the glass. She took a cautious sip and
choked on a giggle and the distinctive sting of
vodka. She looked at him, eyes dancing with
mirth and accusation. "Where did you—"

He affected a very sober face and laid his finger
aside his mouth in a warning gesture. Then, very
elaborately, he opened his jacket a fraction to reveal the top of a flat silver flask in his inside
pocket.

Silver flask. Contraband goods. What else should
she expect from a Regency hero? Meredith tried
to disguise with a laugh the fact that her eyes, with
a perverse will of their own, seemed to be far
more interested in the slim sweep of male hip and
thigh revealed by the opening of his jacket than in
the hidden flask. "What are you," she challenged
lightly, "the town drunk or something?" Nice
thighs, she thought. Very nice. She wondered
how tall he was.

His features relaxed into an easy grin, and he
took up his own drink, which Meredith now realized was a screwdriver. "Nope," he admitted,
"just the town free spirit." He lifted his glass to
her, eyes sparkling. "To the Twenty-first Amend-
ment."

Meredith laughed and touched her glass to his.
He wasn't built like a big man, but it was impossible to tell when he was sitting down like this, his
heels hooked on the rung of the barstool, the
jacket covering up his most interesting features.
From what she could tell, he was slim, compact
and tightly structured, not very muscular, not
very broad. With her luck, he would stand up, and

she would be three inches taller. Not that it mattered, she assured herself quickly, and focused her attention on the glass in her hand as she took another sip. She had been caught staring again.

"My name is Mark Brasfield," he introduced himself gallantly, and extended his hand. The twinkle was in his eyes again, registering acknowledgment of her latest speculations about him. "Your conspirator in crime and always at your service."

It was hard to keep her smile merely polite as Meredith glanced back at him. He seemed to have a way of making her forget her reservations, her caution, even the embarrassment she should have felt every time that knowing light sparkled in his eyes. He made her want to relax with him and smile welcome at him and let herself feel completely at ease. And that was ridiculous, of course. Meredith Griffin had far more class, and more wisdom, than to flirt with a stranger at a bar, even if it was a juice bar and even if the stranger was the best thing she had seen all day.

"Meredith Griffin," she responded, and accepted his offered hand. It was soft and smooth, but the grip was surprisingly firm. And warm. She did not miss the way he caressed her wrist with his thumb for just a moment before releasing her hand, and it made her skin tingle. She immediately put her hand in her lap and turned her attention back to her drink.

"Do they call you Meredith," he inquired, "or is it Merry?"

"Merry," she answered. And so what was the

harm, she rationalized, in making casual conversation? Who knew? The man might be useful to
her. He was a resident. He knew the area and the
people, and he could very probably make things
easier for her. Roger had warned her she could
not expect to just sail in there and demand a con-
frontation. These people, he had cautioned her,
had to be treated very carefully. It couldn't hurt to
be acquainted with a member of the community.
At the very least, Mark could give her proper directions.

She expected him to ask where she was from,
what she was doing there, to continue to make
light, meaningless cocktail-party conversation, to
follow the course of the flirtation to its natural
conclusion. She did not expect him to get to the
point so quickly. "Are you dining alone tonight,
Merry?" he inquired.

"Well, yes..."

"So am I." He rose with sudden decision and
touched her shoulder lightly, indicating she should
do the same. "And I think we'd have a lot better
chance of getting a table if we were a party of two
instead of two parties of one, don't you?"

"Well, I—"

Nothing in his previous manner had given
Meredith cause to suspect he was a man of such
quick action and compelling decisiveness. She did
not even know how it happened, but she was on
her feet, her drink in her hand, his hand firmly
and possessively on her back, and he was guiding
her across the lounge toward the restaurant. They
were halfway across the room before Meredith
got hold of her senses again, and she stopped.

"Wait a minute," she complained, "I don't remember agreeing—"

His eyes were wide with mock innocence. "You can't mean to say you like eating alone?"

There was something about his compelling gaze that made Meredith stammer. He was, in fact, two inches taller than she, and for a woman of five feet ten inches in her stocking feet, that was something of a pleasant shock in itself. It was probably a mixture of that, the endearing way he cocked his head with the question and the warm imprint of his hand on her back that was playing such unaccustomed havoc with Meredith's composure. She had to take a breath to remember what she meant to say, and then the effort registered as a scowl on her face. "It's not that," she told him firmly. "It's just that..." Now her eyes skated away from his briefly. "I'm not so sure this is a good idea."

"Why not?" he demanded with every pretense of genuine confusion.

"Because," she returned, bringing her eyes back to him evenly, "I feel like I'm being picked up."

And then he totally disarmed her with a quick wink and an increased pressure on her shoulder blade, urging her forward. "Don't worry," he told her easily, "you are."

Merry was for a moment too startled to even laugh.

Mark had secured from the hostess a table for two, and they were seated in a corner with menus placed before them before Meredith had recovered herself sufficiently to make objection. By then, of course, her protests were slightly less than convincing, even to her own ears. It was hard even to make her tone severe. "I hope you're not getting the wrong idea," she began.

Mark glanced up from the menu absently. "About what?"

"You—me..." She gestured inadequately. "Having dinner together. I never intended—"

"Oh, I see." Mark assumed a very sober demeanor and closed the menu over his forefinger. In the brighter light of the restaurant she could see that his hair was really closer to mahogany than brown, and with his gray eyes, it was a striking combination. Maybe that was what gave him that touch of something just a little bit out of the ordinary. "The wrong idea—as in picking a girl up at a bar, taking her to dinner, taking her home, taking her to bed...?"

Merry's eyes widened with a mixture of astonishment and laughter, and she managed a rather choked "Something like that!"

Mark's eyes were flecked with outrageous laughter, and a dry twitch of his lips suggested the mockery was directed at himself as much as anyone else. "No problem," he answered. "Things like that simply do not happen around here. I think it's against the law or something." Mark opened his menu again and hid his expression behind his thoughtful perusal of it. "Besides," he added, "it's an hour and a half past my dinnertime, and I'm not scheduling that far in advance. The shish kebab is really good here. So is the snapper."

Merry leaned back in her chair, looking at him, and she could not prevent the small shake of her head or the incredulous amusement that lightened her eyes. Mark Brasfield was definitely the most interesting thing that had happened to her all day—her unfortunate first impression of the township not excluded. It only disturbed her slightly that he might even be the most interesting thing that had happened to her ever. "Do you do this sort of thing often?" she inquired mildly, folding her arms across her chest in amused condescension.

He glanced up at her with another disconcerting wink. "Every chance I get," he assured her. "What about you?"

"Not often enough," she replied, and the quick lightening and softening of his eyes made her wish she had held back a little on the flirting. Mark closed the menu, and Merry quickly opened hers, because she had the most absurd impression that he was about to reach for her hand. She sensed strongly that playfulness with this man could quickly escalate out of control, and she had to remind herself to be careful.

The restaurant, like the lounge, was not lavish but very nice. The tables were set with white linen and cloth napkins with a single silk rose as the centerpiece on each one. The lighting was very bright and the atmosphere more homey than intimate. The diners were subdued and well-mannered; all the men were wearing jackets and dress shirts buttoned at the collar; all the women, modest tailored dresses.

The menus were heavy white vellum embossed with the gold hotel logo, and the selection was quite interesting, though not very varied. There seemed to be an abundance of salads and vegetarian dishes and very few meat entrées. "I don't think I've ever been to a restaurant before," Merry murmured, searching the listing, "that didn't have sirloin on the menu. I'm really in the mood for a thick steak."

"Try the shish kebab," Mark suggested.

As the waitress was already poised to take their order, Meredith shrugged and agreed. Mark placed the order for two salads with house dressing, shish kebab and wild rice and, with an inquiring glance at Merry, coffee. And as the smiling waitress prepared to depart, he added blandly, "Separate checks, please." He glanced at Merry with a tolerant twinkle. "Just so you don't get the wrong idea."

Meredith hid a tightening smile with her knuckles.

"So," Mark inquired, settling back in his chair, "how do you like our gentle little town so far?"

Meredith lifted one eyebrow, even as her forehead furrowed in confusion. It was a charming expression, a trademark characteristic of which Merry was not even aware, but Mark registered it with a subtle lightening of his eyes and a softening of the corner of his lips. "I'm not sure," she admitted. "I got a pretty rude welcome when I first arrived, and to tell the truth, I was almost ready to turn and run the other way."

Now it was Mark's turn to look puzzled. "Oh? What happened?"

"Well, there was this mean old man at the gas station," Merry answered, trying to minimize the episode to its proper proportions, "and then, when I stopped at the first motel, the lady wouldn't even register me. Practically told me to get out of town before sundown."

Mark's troubled expression cleared with a light laugh. Merry liked the way he laughed. So many men could not carry off a laugh well; it usually came out either too boisterous or too forced. But Mark laughed as though he were used to doing it; it was a soft and natural and easy sound, and it made Merry relax. "That's old Maud," he explained. "Not the Chamber of Commerce's favorite citizen. She likes to think she can pick and choose her customers. I wouldn't be surprised," he confided, "if she weren't running some kind of illegal operation out there."

Of course. The old woman was running a roadhouse or a bordello—or even serving booze in a dry county—and she was afraid the very next stranger might be the one to turn her in. She probably made her living off teenagers who checked in without luggage and businessmen out for a quick "lunch" with their secretaries. It was perfectly plausible, and the solving of the mystery took such a burden from Meredith's mind that she felt her whole attitude toward the day change. The smile of relief that lightened her eyes was benevolent and unpreventable.

Mark watched her changing expression with an easy appreciation in his own, and Meredith was fascinated by his face. It was strong and angular, yet not harsh; forceful but gentle. His was a face capable of expressing a multitude of emotions with little effort at all, yet, contrarily, one accustomed to disguising those emotions with every device at his disposal. His eyes smiled, but his lips did not. Or his lips curved indulgently, and his eyes remained alert and curious. When he looked at her sometimes, as he did now, his entire face seemed to soften, but not a single actual muscle moved.

The mouth was most interesting. That little line of cynicism intrigued her, drawing attention to his lips as though it were a deliberate device designed to do so. And when Meredith looked at his lips, she could not help wondering, so far in the back of her mind that it hardly registered at all, whether, when they touched a woman, they would reflect the gentleness and the softness of their appearance or the hardness of the personality she felt certain lurked just below the surface. Sometimes when she looked at those lips, she felt a tingling sensation in her stomach with the curiosity.

All these details Merry had observed in less than an hour's acquaintance, but the most important facet of his face she could not even analyze. It was that when he looked at her, something about her seemed to open to him and to be understood by him. He looked at her as though he had known her for a long time, and the defenses and circuitous games that usually lay between strangers seemed redundant and silly. That unsettled Meredith, because she did not know quite how to deal with it.

Mark said now, easily, "Anyway, Maud's place is on the outskirts of town, so we really can't be held responsible for her inhospitable behavior. How did you like it once you got into town?"

Meredith watched his long fingers curve around his glass; she did not follow the drink's progress to his lips but laughed a little nervously and busied herself with stirring the mixture in her own glass. "Quite a change!" she admitted. "And a surprise." He cocked an eyebrow inquiringly, and she explained, "I didn't expect it to be this big, for one thing, with a real hotel and everything. At most, I was expecting one red light and a general store. The area is pretty rural."

"We're not all that big," Mark protested, "just well developed." And he grinned. "Four red lights."

There were other comments Meredith could have made about her first impression of the town, but they were vague and instinctual feelings that she could not even put into words. A bar that did not serve alcohol, a restaurant that did not serve steak, ingratiating smiles on clear young faces—all perfectly innocent things and nothing to complain about, but somehow, in combination, they served to make Meredith uneasy. And she could hardly judge an entire town by a couple of hours spent in a single hotel. But somehow the entire atmosphere—the bright, homey lighting, the conservatively dressed guests, the subdued conversation—seemed preprogrammed, sterile, not quite real. It was nothing Meredith could put her finger on, but she felt uncomfortable despite the fact that no one at the hotel had so far done anything to make her feel so. It probably had to do with nothing more than the fact that she was the only woman in the room wearing slacks and that her feminine vanity was acting up.

At any rate, Mark seemed to have a well-developed sense of proprietary pride in his town, and she would not have dared to suggest anything that wasn't completely complimentary. She asked instead, "Have you lived here all your life?"

Mark laughed. "You mean you can't tell? I thought I had 'Wall Street' stamped on my forehead."

"So that's it!" Merry exclaimed. That was what made him stand out from the crowd, that little hint of something different about him in the cut of his clothes, the style of his hair, the way he carried himself. And she had no need to explain it to him. He nodded with an amused twinkle in his eye.

"You can take the boy out of the stock market, but you can't take the stock market out of the boy," he said. And he took another sip of his drink. "I left the good life for the easy life about two years ago," he explained, "and decided to go into private business management. Twice the money, half the stress. What about you? What do you do?"

Merry would have liked to have known more

about him, what had led to his defection from international finance, how he had chosen this remote area of the world in which to settle, what kind of work he did now. The more she learned about him, the more she wanted to know. That was not a good sign. She was only going to be there a few days, with any luck at all, and there was no point in becoming interested in this man and even less point in letting her interest show. So she lifted one shoulder lightly and answered with a grin, "I'm an administrative assistant for a legal firm—a glorified secretary. I do all the work; they get all the pay."

Mark cocked his head thoughtfully. "Now, that's funny. On first glance, I would have taken you for a woman who gave the orders, not took them."

A very perceptive comment. For some reason Meredith was not surprised by that. She would not be surprised by anything this man said or did; that was how comfortable she already felt with him. "I was in prelaw," she admitted.

"What happened?"

This time the lift of her shoulders was slightly uncomfortable, although she tried to hide it with a wry smile. "I'm not very big on stress, either." And she felt compelled to add, almost defensively, "Of course, my parents define that characteristic as 'irresponsible' and 'lazy.'" She shrugged, making light of it. "They seem to think that just because I've had eight jobs in six years, I lack a certain amount of staying power. I guess I'm not very ambitious."

At first she had no earthly idea why she should tell him all this, but when Mark smiled, she knew. Just like that, he understood. Meredith's parents had not understood. Her professors had not understood. Even Roger, to whom she had explained in no uncertain terms when she applied for a position with his firm that she had no aspirations beyond the outer office, still inquired persistently when she was going to finish her education. None of them could relate to the fact that knowing one's own limits was just as important as material success, if not more so. Meredith was happy being someone's assistant. She did not want the responsibility, the work load or the command decisions of being in charge. She preferred being behind the scenes to center stage, and she had never had a moment's regret about her career choice. But no one could understand why the star student of her law class had abandoned prestige and success for contentment—until now. Something warm flowed through Meredith, and she smiled at the man who sat across the table from her.

The salads were served then, and the strange moment of rapport between them was broken. It was probably just as well.

Mark picked up the conversation easily in a moment. "Are you planning to stay awhile or just passing through?"

"A few days," Merry conceded.

"Good." He gave her a disconcerting little wink. "I'd hate to think one crazy old lady could put you off this part of the country entirely. Besides, you can't really make a fair judgment from a couple of hours inside a hotel, can you? You might even like it here."

Merry paused with her fork midway to her lips, a puzzled smile etching her features. "How did you know that? That I'd only been here a few hours?"

He leaned back and touched his napkin to his lips, his eyes glinting with self-satisfied mischief. "The ways in which I gain access to information about tall blond strangers in town are strictly top secret," he assured her, "but totally reliable."

She lowered her fork to her salad bowl with a skeptical look, and he relented, chuckling. "Simple deduction," he answered. "If you had been here for any length of time, you would have known to make reservations for dinner here on Friday night. And you wouldn't ask so many questions. And—" The slow, confident light that came into his eyes affected Merry peculiarly; it made her forget completely that his previous two explanations were incredibly lame. "I would have met you long before now."

"Oh, you would, would you?" Merry tilted her head flirtatiously. She could feel the brightening of her eyes, the appealing color of her skin, the little tingle of adrenaline that always accompanied the boy-meets-girl game. And she was enjoying it. "You sound as though you have the technique down pat."

"The bachelor's survival kit," he admitted modestly. "The social life in this town is not terribly exciting, so we have to be inventive about ways to entertain ourselves."

Merry's lips tightened disapprovingly, although the sparkle in her eyes was totally contradictory. "Like trolling for women in hotel lounges?"

Mark's expression immediately changed to mock insult and disappointment. "You make it sound so tacky."

"It's not?" she challenged archly.

"Not," he argued convincingly, "when it's done with refinement and taste."

Meredith couldn't help laughing. "You think you're very clever, don't you?"

The slightest hint of an enigmatic smile curved his lips; it fascinated Merry. "I profess to a modest skill," he agreed. "For example, look how much I've learned about you in less than an hour. Why, already we have the basis for a deep and meaningful relationship."

It was a teasing comment, but for just a second it took Meredith aback. For just the briefest of moments she imagined she was in another place, under different circumstances, and that such a thing might really be possible. She recovered herself by quickly taking a sip of her drink. "So you know I'm a law-school dropout turned secretary." She shrugged casually. "That I've only been in town a few hours and that I like Bloody Marys with vodka—hardly enough to qualify you as a master of observation."

"Aha," he responded with a mischievous quirk of his brow. "The lady challenges me." He leaned forward with his arms crossed lightly on the table, directing her with a subtly amused, easily assessing gaze. "You come from an upper-middle-class

family, with very stable, career-oriented parents.
You had trouble learning to write in school and
probably caused your parents a lot of grief with
low grades for your first three academic years.
You've never been married. You like to play tennis and swim. You should wear glasses, but you're
too vain. You took ballet as a young child and
hated it... What's the matter? Am I going too
fast for you?"

Meredith stared at him, openmouthed, completely astounded. She lowered her glass very
slowly to the table again. "Good... heavens," she
managed weakly. If he had not looked so innocently amused, she would have been genuinely
frightened. "Are you psychic or something? How
did you..."

He leaned back, eyes snapping self-confident
approval with her reaction even as his lips curved
into a relenting smile. "Only an upper-middle-
class family could afford to send their daughter to
law school," he explained smugly. "Most left-
handed people have trouble learning to write, and
it usually affects their grades in the early years.
There's no sign that you've ever worn a wedding
ring on your left hand—although that was a long
shot," he admitted. "If you'd only been married a
few months, the ring wouldn't have left a mark.
However—" And then he surprised her by reaching forward and taking her hand lightly in his,
turning it palm upward. Meredith did not know
whether the sudden slight jump of her pulse was
due to the unexpected gesture or to the startling
nature of his accurate observations. "These slight

calluses here—'' he brushed his thumb over her palm, a warm touch that made her fingers curl ''—could only have been caused by a tennis racket. And your upper arms are firm, your shoulders straight—the swimmer's posture. And that tiny little line over your nose?'' Again, he surprised her by reaching up and brushing his forefinger across the bridge of her nose. His smile was gentle. ''Eyestrain.''

He settled back but did not release her hand. Meredith knew she should pull away, but she didn't. She swallowed to clear her throat and to calm an uncertain fluttering there; she made her tone light. ''And the ballet lessons?''

''You were tall as a girl,'' he answered. ''Your parents probably thought it would give you grace. But because you were tall, you felt awkward. You couldn't do the steps; you hated ballet.''

Meredith's laugh was nervous. Still he held her hand, very lightly, across the table. ''Well, bravo! I'm impressed, and I take back any slighting remarks I may have made about your, er, skill.'' Skill was exactly the word, she realized suddenly. Gentle eyes, entrancing secret smile, impossible charm—this man was a real professional. And the soft, almost absent circular motions Mark's thumb was tracing on her palm were making her whole body warm.

With a quick smile, Merry pulled her hand away, and he offered no resistance. The waitress was approaching with their plates, and Merry wondered if that was not the primary reason she decided to break the physical contact. She could not help feeling self-conscious about holding hands with a perfect stranger in a public restaurant. But that was the only unpleasant sensation associated with the contact.

The shish kebab was very good despite the fact that the skewer was decorated with far more vegetables than meat. It was, however, served with a spicy wild rice mixture and the most delicious rich brown rolls and butter that Merry had ever tasted. Mark told her they baked their own bread there, and the butter was fresh from the dairy a few miles out of town.

As they ate, they talked—or at least Mark talked; Merry was too hungry to do much to keep up her side of the conversation, and afterward she would realize with some amazement how little he had actually said about himself, the town in which he lived or anything else of much importance. Yet she found herself drawn to the sound of his voice, fascinated by the movements of his hands and his face, delighting in his easy laughter and the quick sparks of mirth in his eyes. He conducted himself with the unaffected charm of a man who has never met a stranger, yet there was a contrary sense of contained power behind every move and gesture, an alertness, a keen intelligence behind the laughing façade of his eyes that seemed to give him the ability to observe and absorb every detail about his opponent while revealing nothing of himself. That characteristic both disturbed and intrigued Meredith.

It also unsettled her that within the space of one shared dinner hour she felt more at ease with him, and more attracted to him, than surely was practical. Meredith was not a person who let down her guard easily, but with this man she had never even raised it. It was just that she was tired, she assured herself. It was just that it had been a long, tense day topped off by two very unpleasant episodes, and she was merely relieved to relax with a friendly face.

Under other circumstances she probably wouldn't even have noticed the infinitesimal deepening of laugh lines when his eyes smiled but his lips did not or the way he touched the corner of his lips when he was serious or the slim strength of long fingers. She wouldn't have noticed the way his formfitted shirt hugged his chest when his jacket parted and he leaned back, and her eyes would not have repeatedly traveled to his throat, silently urging his fingers to reach up and casually undo the high button there.

The warmth and ease of companionship she felt with him was no doubt just a trick of the imagination. The attraction she felt for him was no more than predictable, for he exuded a quiet confidence and a low-key sexuality that was hard to resist. But Meredith had been attracted to men on first sight before, and she knew nothing had to come of it. Under other circumstances— Well, under other circumstances she might have viewed the entire matter differently, but the fact was that this was a chance encounter with no potential for anything more. They had enjoyed dinner and each other's company; they would pay their separate checks and go their separate ways. They might smile at each other if they happened to pass on the street during the short time she was there, but that was all. All that was left for Meredith to do was enjoy the moment while it lasted and take it for what it was worth.

Because she was feeling festive for some reason and because she wanted to prolong the meal a little longer, Merry asked for a dessert menu when the ineffably smiling waitress came to remove their plates and refill their coffee cups. And she saw the same look of apology and chagrin cross the young woman's face as was on the bartender's when she had had the temerity to ask for vodka in her Bloody Mary.

"I'm sorry, ma'am," the waitress replied timidly. "We don't have desserts."

Meredith stared at her, unable to conceal her surprise. But there was hardly any point in questioning or complaining, so she merely shrugged. "It's probably just as well. I'm on a diet."

"Aren't we all?" agreed Mark, and the waitress looked relieved as she placed their checks before them.

Despite his earlier resolve, Merry half expected Mark to try to pay for her dinner. She was both amused and relieved when he did not. The time they had spent together had only felt like a date; in fact, they were only two strangers sharing a table, and Mark had the distinction clear, even if Merry did not.

Only when she felt his hand lightly on her back as they left the restaurant, it started to feel like a date again. To distract herself from the way the warmth of his fingers just beneath her shoulder blade seemed to be heating the skin all over her body, Meredith said, "That was a delicious dinner, but diet or no diet, I think it's pretty cruel of them not to serve desserts. What's the fun of being away from home if you can't live it up a little?"

"I know of a great place for ice cream," Mark suggested.

They were in the lobby now, standing beneath the artificial shelter of a potted palm, and Meredith turned to him, the eagerness in her eyes only partly feigned. Another hour with him over ice cream or coffee or whatever was available was a prospect with definite appeal. She simply did not want to end the evening so soon.

Mark let his hand drop from her back, but his fingers trailed lightly around her shoulder and down her arm and stopped with a very light brushing motion against her elbow, as though, he, too, did not want to sever the contact so quickly. His smile was gentle and teasing, but the light in his eyes seemed to focus directly on the rhythm of her heart. "My place," he offered simply.

Meredith had to drop her eyes because she was very much afraid her initial reaction would reveal exactly how tempted she was by his half-serious offer. "Thanks," she murmured demurely, but her cheeks still felt warm. "I think I'd better stick to my diet."

He looked at her for a moment longer, smiling, neither surprised nor disappointed. She liked him because she knew the pass had not been entirely serious and because, in making it, he had let her know that the strange attraction she had been feeling for him all evening was not entirely one-sided. She liked him because that gentle light in his eyes told her how much he wished she had said yes and because his next words were easy and natural, allowing no awkwardness to develop from the subtle awareness that was beginning to pulse between them. "Maybe tomorrow you'll let me show you around town a little," he said. "This is a nice part of the country—a lot different from Oregon, but I think you'll like it. Who knows," he suggested with a twinkle, "you might even decide to stay awile."

Meredith found it a lot easier to laugh than she had supposed. Something about the way he was looking at her and the light, warm touch of his fingers on her arm were making her throat tight. "Who knows?" she agreed recklessly. "It certainly seems like a nice little town."

"It is," he assured her. "Despite the fact," Mark added, and his voice softened a fraction and his eyes seemed to gentle and deepen with question, "that the nights have a tendency to be long and lonely."

Merry maintained that gaze for just a moment, and she did not have to strain very hard to read the suggestion behind his words. For the briefest of seconds she thought about it, and it made her mouth dry. Under other circumstances, maybe...

Meredith swallowed; she trained her lips into a semblance of a polite smile. "It was nice meeting you, Mark," she said. "Thanks for keeping me company during dinner."

Even as the gentle curve of his lips accepted her refusal, his eyes held hers. "My pleasure entirely," he answered, and she thought he really meant it. And then his fingers traveled upward to clasp a strand of thick, straight blond hair as it fell over her shoulder, and his eyes followed the movement. His face seemed to soften, and his voice was a little husky as he inquired, "Are you sure you won't change your mind about that ice cream? Chocolate chip."

The spark in his eyes was more than teasing this time, and Meredith tried very hard to pretend she did not notice. Again she smiled, and his fingers fell slowly away from her hair. "Good night, Mark," she said.

His smile was regretful but not discouraged. "I'll see you in the morning, Merry."

The promise, unexpected and totally pleasurable, seemed to sweep Merry along in euphoria all the way up the stairs. It wasn't a terrible place, after all. She wasn't going to hate every minute she was there.

Of course she hadn't come there for frivolity, and she had to remind herself severely that too much was at stake there for her to allow herself to be sidetracked by some good-looking local resident. But Merry was used to taking every advantage life had to offer, and was there any rule against making the time she had to spend there as pleasant as possible?

Meredith fell asleep in the strange bed a lot

more easily than she had expected to, no longer dreading the morning but actually looking forward to it. Yes, this place was a lot different from Oregon, but it didn't have to be all bad.

It was a very long time later that it occurred to Meredith that she had never told Mark she was from Oregon. By that time, it hardly seemed to make any difference.

Chapter Three

The morning caught Meredith unprepared, coming, as mornings had a tendency to do for her, a lot sooner than she had expected. She was sprawled facedown across the roomy bed, covers tangled around the lace hems of her silky pajamas, her face completely obscured by a strawlike tumble of hair, when a surprised feminine voice said above her, "Oh! Excuse me."

Meredith opened one eye a crack and peered through the brown-gold veil at the dim figure of a woman in a maid's uniform beside her bed. She gave an undignified grunt, pushed her hair out of her eyes and turned over. After a moment of blinking stupidly at the unfamiliar surroundings, she sat up, pulling the covers around her. Gradually, orientation began to return. The pretty peach-and-green room. The town of Stonington, Kansas. The friendly hotel where everyone was under twenty-five and no one ever stopped smiling. Bloody Marys and ice cream. Mark Brasfield.

Merry turned to the embarrassed young maid,

who explained quickly, "I'm terribly sorry. I thought you had gone down for breakfast. But there was a package for you." She thrust the plain brown package at Merry with an apologetic smile. "I'll come back and do the room later," she assured her and was gone before Merry could even thank her.

Now fully awake, Meredith got out of bed, curiously studying the package, wondering what time it was. Who would send her a package there? No one even knew where she was. She had never gotten around to calling her parents again the previous night, so they had no idea whether or not she had even arrived, much less which hotel she was at. Merry tried not to let alarm tinge her curiosity as she searched into her handbag for a pair of nail clippers with which to cut the twine.

She snipped away the twine impatiently and tore off the paper. She lifted the lid and then sat back, a secret smile of amusement and delight brightening the whole room. Inside the box, nestled in mounds of tissue paper, was a fifth of vodka. Taped to the label was a note that said, "For those long lonely nights—Mark."

She was hard put not to laugh out loud. I'll see you in the morning, he had said. Was he at that moment waiting downstairs?

Merry jumped up quickly and started for the closet. A glance at the watch she had left on the night table showed her it was already ten o'clock, and he had said morning.

But then she stopped, embarrassed by her schoolgirlish eagerness, firmly reminding herself that she was there for a reason, not for a vacation. Mark Brasfield was charming, attractive and probably the most interesting man she had met in a long time. He was every woman's romantic hero, almost too good to be true, and of course the temptation he offered was hard to resist. But Meredith was supposed to be a sensible woman, and she could not afford to be distracted by him. She had things to do, and the sooner she accomplished them, the sooner she could put her parents' minds—and her own—at rest. The sooner she accomplished them, the sooner she could leave there . . . and Mark.

Her brow twisted into that unconscious little gesture of amusement and puzzlement with the thought and the unexpected emotions it caused. It was silly, of course. She had only met the man one time. The reluctance she felt over the fact that their acquaintanceship must of necessity be a short one was totally uncalled for. Then, with a breath and a squaring of her shoulders, she dismissed the sparkling gray eyes of Mark Brasfield and sat down at the desk to dial her parents' phone number.

Her mother answered on the second ring, and the relief and hope in her mother's voice was enough to completely banish all frivolous thoughts from Meredith's mind. Her parents were depending on her. This was a serious matter. They had been driven to the point of desperation over the past year, and Meredith's decision to go to Stonington had brought them their first real glimmer of hope for a cause that had so far met with nothing but defeat. Meredith was ashamed of herself for not calling them the night before, after she returned from dinner; she felt guilty for the few hours of carefree fun she had spent with Mark and even worse for allowing thoughts of him to distract her that morning.

"Have you seen him yet?" her mother wanted to know, and the note of eagerness and hope in her voice went straight to Meredith's heart.

"No, Mom," she replied gently, "not yet. I didn't get in until late last night, but I'm going to call over there today."

"I know he'll see you, Merry," her mother said with a quiet, almost desperate conviction. "You were always so close. Kevin hardly even knew Roger, so naturally ..."

The voice trailed off into things that couldn't be said, things the two women shared in thought but would never put into words. There was no guarantee that Kevin would see his sister. There was no guarantee that he had even had the chance to refuse to see Roger. It was more than possible that Kevin had never been told of Roger's visit and that he wouldn't be told about his sister's. There was even the possibility—an awful outside cognizance that none of them would consciously admit to themselves—that Kevin was no longer alive to make the choice.

Merry had not yet opened the heavy draperies to admit the morning sunshine, and the dim glow of the lamp by which she sat seemed suddenly a very frail protection against the shadows that crowded the room. She shivered in her thin pajamas, but she allowed no trace of it to filter into her voice. "Don't worry, Mom," she said firmly. "He'll see me. It just may take a few days, that's all. You know what Roger said—we have to move slowly."

The word Roger had used was "carefully," but Meredith did not want to quote him exactly to her mother. They had enough to worry about as it was.

"Okay, Merry." Meredith could hear the smile that was being forced into her mother's voice—an occurrence so common that Merry did not even have to close her eyes to visualize her mother's face. Forced smiles, desperate eyes, strained hope, lines of aging, had all become part of her mother's countenance in the past year. "I know you'll do the best thing, sweetheart."

Merry had to swallow to clear her throat against the sudden moist lump there, and even then it was a moment before she could speak. *I know you'll do the best thing*... She could not remember either of her parents ever voicing such confidence in her. No, Merry did not do the best thing; she did the easiest thing, the quickest thing, the most self-gratifying thing. But now, just this once, she had a chance to act on behalf of someone other than herself. For this one time, she would do the right thing, the noble thing, the courageous thing. And her parents would be proud of her.

"Take care, Mom," she managed at last, softly.

"You, too, Merry."

Meredith replaced the receiver slowly, deep in thought. She wondered what the chances were that she would be able to see Kevin. She wondered what she would find if she did. And she wondered what she would do—what she was supposed to do—after she had talked to him.

"Oh, damn it, Kevin," she whispered out loud, and thrust her fingers through her tangled hair, pushing it back from her face. "How did this ever happen to you? Why did you let it happen to us?"

She got up restlessly and went to draw the draperies. The morning sun was high and gentle, and her second-floor window looked down on the park, a view that had been promised her the night before by the desk clerk. It was a pretty little square of greenery in the middle of town, shaded with budding elms and pink-blossomed cherry trees that must have been maintained at enormous cost, bright with colorful flower beds of waxy tulips and crocus. There was a wishing well in the center, and an occasional figure strolled by leisurely, enjoying the morning sun. A quiet little town. A peaceful place. The turmoil and distress that had brought Merry there seemed harshly at odds with the demeanor of the town itself.

Meredith dressed in jeans and a lightweight, cowl-necked sweater, anxious for a cup of coffee before she started the day. Roger had said the best thing to do was to phone the institute and make an appointment with the Reverend Samuels. He, in turn, would arrange a meeting with Kevin. "Try going through channels first," Roger had emphasized. "These people don't take kindly to outsiders breaking their rules. You're going to need all the cooperation you can get."

Meredith had promised she would try it his way. But they both knew she wasn't much of one for abiding by the rules.

But this time you will, she scolded herself as she ran the hairbrush through her thick, straight hair. *This time you'll do exactly what's expected of you. You'll call up this Samuels character, and you'll be polite, proper and patient. You'll do what he tells you to do. You'll play it his way. Too much is at stake here for you to blow it with a temper tantrum.*

She applied a touch of beige shadow to her lids, darkened her lashes with mascara and brushed a hint of blusher over her cheekbones, rubbing it in with her fingers. As she colored her lips with a glossy, vibrant coral and folded a saucy paisley scarf into a headband that knotted just below her left ear, she refused to admit that the reason she was taking so much care with her appearance that morning was the slight chance that Mark might still be downstairs.

Mark was not downstairs—or if he was, Merry did not see him. The dining room was not very crowded, but the few people who lingered there did favor her with guarded curious glances. Again Merry felt that self-conscious uneasiness over the way she was dressed, followed quickly by a flash of annoyance. If the hotel was so high-class that they did not allow jeans in the dining room, they could damn well post a notice saying so.

The hostess was ready to greet her with that same effusive smile that seemed to be standard equipment for hotel employees. Meredith started to follow her to the table and then was distracted by a brochure stand at the entrance to the dining room she had not noticed the night before. With a leap of excitement, she picked one up. It was a pamphlet on the Source of Enlightenment.

The sensations that churned in Meredith's stomach as she absently took the table the hostess indicated were a mixture of eagerness, anger and revulsion. The colorful glossy folder she held in her hand advertised the breaking hearts and homes, the waste of young minds, the source of her family's misery for the past year and the reason Meredith was there. She looked at it for a moment, trying to subdue the conflicting and energy-consuming emotions, before opening it to scan the inside.

Meredith did not know why she was surprised at the commerciality of the brochure. The front of it showed a side view of a well-landscaped, architecturally modern structure with many wings and angles. The caption read: the Temple of Enlightenment. Inside was a brief history of the organization: begun in 1960 with one man's dream for spiritual fulfillment, growing throughout the years to spread the light of true contentment to millions around the world. And on to a brief description of life inside the commune, where thousands of devotees chose to make the temple in Stonington, or others like it across the country, their permanent domicile, growing their own food, weaving their own cloth, studying the teachings of Enlightenment and living in perfect harmony with nature and themselves. There followed an outline of the philosophy and teachings of the cult, filled with subtle propaganda and catchwords such as "inner awareness" and "cosmic truths," and Meredith felt such a surge of brief, fierce hatred that tears stung her eyes and she could no longer see the words.

Pictures of Kevin flashed through her mind. A gentle, sober little boy with big brown eyes that too easily filled with hurt. A quiet, thoughtful teenager who was always just a little out of step with his peer group. While other boys were out on dates, Kevin was at home reading. When other boys were chortling in the garage over pornographic magazines, Kevin was busy mowing the lawn of the old lady next door—without asking for or expecting payment. Other boys were into drugs and fast cars; Kevin rode his bicycle until he was seventeen. Kevin, a studious young man always ready with a quick smile or calm advice, an honors student in premed at the university; he was everything Merry was not. He was her parents' pride and joy.

He was gentle, considerate, intelligent, introspective and quietly ambitious. He was tall and good-looking, with a quirky sense of humor and a smile that could melt the heart of any female within firing distance. He always knew the right thing to say, and he always cared about what other people were saying. He had never disappointed anyone in his life. His teachers loved him. Old ladies and little children loved him. And Meredith loved him. But he had been stolen from them. His life had been ripped away, and it didn't even belong to him anymore.

"It's not fair," Meredith muttered fiercely to herself, and her hand closed around the brochure until the corners crumpled. "They can't do this...."

"That's what I like," said a cheerful voice over her shoulder. "A woman who's a good conversationalist."

Mark Brasfield pulled out a chair and sat across from her.

Merry was too distracted to even be embarrassed at having been caught talking to herself for the second time. She merely composed her face the best she could, gave him a fair semblance of a welcoming smile, and said, "Hello," then, quickly, "Thanks for the present."

He teased her with a quick wink and replied, "I was counting on your being the type of woman who doesn't like to drink alone."

But even through the light banter his eyes were searching her face; Meredith's wan smile and lack of rejoinder did not help to disguise her mood much. Mark said quietly, "You look upset. Is something wrong?"

Meredith started to shrug and dismiss it, but he had already seen the brochure she was clenching in her hand. And she had no real reason for secrecy. She sighed and began to smooth out the creases made in the folder by her angry fingers. "It's just this—garbage," she said, and did not quite succeed in keeping the venom out of her tone as she thrust it toward him.

Mark glanced at the brochure curiously, then returned it to her with a mild lift of his eyebrow.

"I take it you're not a proponent of religious freedom?"

"This is not *religion*, and you know it!" she flung back at him. Her color was heightening. "It's cult worship; it's brainwashing—"

"That's a matter of opinion, isn't it?" he returned blandly. "I don't doubt the people out at the Source of Enlightenment would have an entirely different point of view."

Merry fell silent, staring at him.

A slow, sympathetic smile curved his lips. "But I do understand what you mean," he assured her gently. "Some of the methods used by these ... organizations ... are not entirely orthodox. But ..." And he shrugged. "We're living in desperate times. Everyone's looking for instant happiness. And as long as it makes people feel better, who are we to judge whether it's right or wrong?"

But Meredith was in no mood to be reasonable, open-minded or philosophical. Obviously, Mark Brasfield had never had the experience with this or any other religious cult suffered by Meredith and her family. He, with his Wall Street manners and his laid-back approach to life, could not possibly understand what Meredith was feeling now. She said shortly, "Do you know anything about this place?"

"Some," he admitted, and his face revealed neither interest nor boredom. "It's hard not to, living here. Why?"

"My brother ..." she began, and then did not know how to put it. My brother is a member of the organization? Is under their spell? Is being held prisoner? "Is there," she finished lamely.

There was no surprise in his expression as he looked at her, only thoughtfulness. That day he was wearing a soft gray sweater that could have been cashmere over a light-colored shirt; it hugged the lines of his chest as he leaned back in the chair, hooking one arm casually over the back. He nodded slowly, understanding. "And that's why you're here," he concluded.

Meredith swallowed back lingering emotion and lowered her eyes. His calm approach to the entire matter made her previous display of passion a little embarrassing. Of course he wouldn't understand how she felt. No outsider could. "No one has seen or heard from him," she said, and her voice sounded a little halting, "in over a year." And now she glanced up at Mark, confident her emotions were under control. "I was hoping to be able to talk to him," she explained.

Again Mark nodded, unsurprised, unimpressed. "The brochure says, 'You are invited to visit our assembly at any time,'" he pointed out. "There should be no problem."

How easy he made it sound. Meredith smiled a little, trying to relax, even allowing herself to believe for the moment that he was right—no problem. "I guess so," she admitted. "It's just that . . ." And she shrugged. "Maybe I'm overreacting to the whole thing."

And Mark sat there, his arm crooked over the back of the chair, looking strong and relaxed and in control, watching her with a gentle, alert perception. "Sometimes," he suggested, "it's hard to let go when people you love decide to follow a path that's different from your own."

Meredith wanted to object that it had not been Kevin's decision, that even if it was, he was wrong, that people should not be allowed to make choices like that. But she knew how foolish and narrow-minded those arguments would sound in the face of such thoughtful concern. Besides, she was touched by the genuine caring that had prompted the observation and was grateful for it. Her hesitant, half-reluctant smile told him so.

The waitress brought them both coffee, and Mark volunteered unexpectedly, "I could take you out there this afternoon if you like."

Meredith paused in the act of stirring cream into her coffee, her face lightening with swift gratitude and relief. "Oh, would you?"

He lifted one shoulder even as the corner of his lips cocked with a half grin. "Actually, I can think of better ways to spend a day," he admitted, "but since the so-called temple is really the only tourist attraction we have around here . . ." He lifted his coffee cup. "Why not?"

And then Merry's face clouded. "I don't think I can see Kevin without an appointment, though."

"If he's one of the Guardians," Mark answered, "probably not."

Meredith's brow puckered with startled confusion, and Mark explained, "Guardians of the Truth." The quirk of his lips that emphasized the cynical line near his mouth held a hint of condescension and self-mockery. "They're like monks; they live in the temple and completely close themselves off to the outside world. It's all in the brochure."

Guardian. Monk. Somehow hearing those words applied to Kevin in such a casual fashion brought it all home to Merry with a sudden clarity that was almost too much to bear, and slow despair filled her. *Oh, Kevin,* she thought. *Sweet, gentle Kevin. Why?*

She was not aware that her pain showed on her face until Mark said quietly, "You're really worried about him, aren't you?"

Meredith swallowed again on the tightening in her throat and nodded. She looked up at Mark, so calm, so self-assured, and it was as though he were inviting her to share her burden and halve it. She could not refuse the comfort he offered. "This past year," she began with difficulty, "since Kevin left—it's been hell on my parents. He was so bright, so promising, so good. . . ." And she broke off with a helpless sigh, curling her fingers around her cup. "I've seen my mother grow old before my very eyes and my father all but lose his reason for living. It's just about destroyed them."

"And you, Merry?" Mark inquired perceptively. "How do you feel about it?"

"He's my brother," she answered simply. "And they're depending on me."

The slight, softening curve of Mark's lips seemed to understand more than she wanted him to know, and Meredith dropped her eyes to her coffee cup. "Anyway," she finished with a determined breath, "I've got to see him, to talk to him—"

"Do you really think he'll come back with you?" Mark inquired gently, cutting straight to the heart of the matter.

Meredith looked up, startled, for she had not gotten that far ahead in her own thinking. She did not know what to say.

"He may not want to," Mark pointed out reasonably.

The small, defiant tilt to her chin was at the same time both courageous and vulnerable. "Then he'll have to tell me that himself," she answered.

There was a softening of Mark's features, even as a spark of what could have been admiration lightened his eye. "Well," he declared, "we'll definitely have to see what we can do to help you out. A face as pretty as yours," he told her, his eyes sweeping her features in a way that brought a warm flush of pleasure to Meredith's cheeks, "shouldn't be marred by worry lines."

Of course it was a blatant line, one that a self-confessed experienced bachelor like Mark must constantly pull from his store at random. But when he said it, he sounded almost believable. He sounded almost sincere. *Feet on the ground, Merry,* she reprimanded herself sternly, and her lips tightened into a tight smile of amused skepticism. "Not pretty," she corrected him. "My face is not pretty. Distinguished, yes, memorable, possibly. Perhaps even—" she tilted her head in an attitude of exaggerated consideration "—handsome. But never pretty."

Mark's brows lifted in mild challenge; his eyes sparkled madly. "I reserve the right to my own opinion," he retorted. "I happen to like strong, aggressive faces. And I think yours is pretty."

Meredith leaned her chin on her fist, meeting his dancing gaze with an even mirth in her own. "And I happen to like being the center of any topic of discussion. Do tell me more."

Mark laughed, his eyes sweeping her with frank approval; he saluted her with his coffee cup. "You're very good at this, aren't you?"

Meredith relaxed and leaned back, taking up her own cup. "What?"

"Flirting," he responded, that easy frank spark of unabashed pleasure still lightening his eyes as he sipped from his cup. "You don't see too much of that around here; it's refreshing."

"Oh, yes," Merry answered, and for just a moment some of the carefree spirit of the conversation went out of her mood. She glanced down at her coffee cup. "I'm good at all sorts of useless, frivolous things." And then, because she was afraid he would pick up the note of self-pity in her tone, she glanced up quickly and said, "Listen, do you think we could go out to the temple now? I mean," she amended hastily, not wanting to appear to be taking advantage of his casual offer, "if you're not busy and if you really don't mind...."

But Mark was already shaking his head. "Open to the public," he quoted, indicated the brochure, "from two to five Saturday afternoons. But I will make good on my offer to show you around town this morning, and we can drive out thereafter lunch, okay?"

For a moment, Meredith hesitated. What he

was suggesting was that they spend the whole day together, and the only thing that made her reluctant was that she could think of nothing she would like better. She wasn't there to have fun. She wasn't there to find new and better ways to meet interesting men. She certainly had no time, and no need, to get involved with this stranger.

But there was nothing she could do until two o'clock. He had been kind enough to offer to take her himself. What was she supposed to do, sit in her room counting the flowers on the wallpaper until the afternoon? She smiled and spread her hands. "Okay. You have yourself one eager-eyed tourist. Entertain me."

The deliberate suggestive twinkle in his eye caused a warm tingle of excitement to begin in Merry's fingers. "Best offer I've had all day," he muttered, and reached for her hand as he stood. "Ready?"

It seemed like the most natural thing in the world for Merry to lace her fingers through his.

Chapter Four

A stroll through a peaceful little middle America town on a spring morning was the perfect prescription for anyone's anxiety, but the fact that it was Mark who was at her side and his fingers that were entwined casually with hers made the exercise far more than soothing for Meredith. The coiled strength of the man who walked beside her reminded Merry of riverboat gamblers and black-hatted desperadoes; the way the light breeze lifted his hair made her think of long strolls through Hyde Park, he in top hat and cane, she in parasol and empire gown. But when the sun-crinkled eyes smiled at her, the leap of excitement that momentarily speeded Merry's pulse brought her back to the present, a real man with a warm strong touch and a confident stride, easy laughter and witty rejoinders, a man she liked more and more with each passing minute.

The town was almost as intriguing a mixture of past and present, contradictions and complexities, as the man who introduced her to it—and just as unfathomable. As Meredith had already begun to suspect, it was much larger than Roger had given her to believe, and even though their tour took them only along the main streets, Merry was impressed. It combined the small-town atmosphere with the bustling encroachment of industrialization in a way that was both amazing and a little bizarre. Interspersed among neatly painted Victorian storefronts and residences that had been converted for office space were low modern buildings with attractively landscaped lawns and modern parking lots. There were four banks and three real-estate offices, all new. Many of the buildings housed branches of large corporations, which surprised Meredith. Mark explained that the town had seen a sudden surge in growth in the past three years, which accounted for the mixture of old and new, and that, indeed, it was still experiencing growing pains. But to Merry the entire town was reminiscent of something from a Ray Bradbury novel.

It was a combination of things, none of them in and of themselves particularly remarkable, but when put together, they merged to form a very unsettling picture. There were no movie theaters. There was not a single bar or nightclub or even a pool hall. And one would think that in a town expanding as fast as this one apparently was, at least one of the fast-food chains would have invaded the territory. All of the modern buildings looked exactly alike: flat, square sandstone structures with two long, narrow windows on either side of the front door. And all the older buildings were painted the same simple unrelenting white. And when Meredith inquired, Mark informed her there was no jail.

There were other things, none of them particularly disturbing by themselves, all of them blending so subtly into what seemed to be the natural atmosphere of the place that it took a while for Meredith to even notice what it was about the mood of this small-town-cum-big-city that bothered her. She did notice right away, however, what seemed to be a preponderance of fresh-faced young men in white collarless tunics with the gold hotel logo emblazoned on the left breast—and their female counterparts, all with long, neatly brushed hair and wearing straight white shifts with the same elliptical symbol woven into the material.

"They're from the church," Mark explained when she questioned. "Representatives, I guess you might call them. You'll see that uniform all over town."

Meredith tried not to let that cast a shadow over her day. She tried not to search each passing face and hope that it was Kevin; she tried not to picture her brother with his beautiful wheat-colored hair cropped off above the ears and his gentle humorous smile changed into the programmed, automatic gesture of faceless contentment. Of course it was only natural that some of the church people would be in town. Where else would they go? She tried to push away that little chill of revulsion that gripped her whenever one passed, and she tried not to think of Kevin.

There were other things, much more subtle, almost too petty to mention, that combined to give Merry a sense of uneasiness. The streets were busy with women doing their Saturday shopping and men waiting patiently for them in the cars or gathering with a group of friends in a doorway or under a budding tree to pass the time of day. Not one of the women—*not a single one*—wore jeans or even slacks. All of them were dressed plainly but neatly in shirtwaists or dark skirts and prim-collared blouses; all hemlines were below the knee, all colors tasteful and understated. Apparently there was no beauty parlor in town, either, for hairstyles were simple, mostly long and braided or bound up in buns or chignons. And none of them wore makeup. Not even lipstick. It was a silly thing, and the only reason it bothered Meredith at all was because she felt so conspicuous in her designer jeans and tight sweater and paisley hair band, not to mention the glossed lips and darkened lashes. She felt like an eighties character in a forties movie.

"Everyone certainly does dress...conservatively," Meredith felt compelled to comment after a time. "Is there some kind of law against women in slacks?"

Mark chuckled. "This is not exactly the fashion center of the Midwest," he admitted.

Meredith tried to shrug it off. "Oh, well. They say the unisex look is on its way out, anyway. I think it has something to do with male fashion designers not being able to tell the difference between themselves and their models. Men prefer women in skirts."

Mark's eyes swept her with an alert, appraising gaze, a suggestive spark lurking just beneath the surface of his thoughtful expression. "Oh, I don't know," he decided. "While a bit of bare calf is appealing every now and then, nothing can complete with a pair of designer jeans when it comes to highlighting a woman's most, er, interesting features."

He had dropped just half a step behind her with the last, and the brush of his gaze across her backside was as palpable and stimulating as a caress. Meredith blushed, for the one thing she could not handle with grace was a remark about her figure. She had always been tall and large-boned, and the stigma of awkwardness that had cursed her in adolescence had left its mark on her adult years. She was sensitive about a figure that was neither round nor cuddly nor, she thought, particularly sexy. From waist to knee she was flat and angular, strong and practical and distinctly unfeminine. There was no alluring dip to her waist, no enticing curve to her derrier, no slim, delicate thighs—none of those things that men were supposed to find so irresistible about a woman. Perhaps she should take a hint from these women and cover her deficit figure with frills and lace, but the comfort of slacks was something she simply could not see herself giving up for anyone.

Mark said now, a little more seriously, "If you didn't bring a dress with you, though, you might want to think about buying one before this afternoon. They're pretty strict about dress codes out at the temple."

Merry stopped and stared at him. "You mean they won't let me in dressed in jeans?"

"Or slacks," he qualified, and then shrugged, pointing out, "Some churches won't let you in unless your head is covered. They all have their little idiosyncrasies."

For a moment the feminist in Meredith rebelled, and her brow gathered into cloudy stubborn lines that Mark seemed to find captivating. Then, with every inch of the struggle with her conscience showing on her face, she relented with a dry grimace. "When in Rome, I guess," she admitted reluctantly. "So where do all these fashion plates we see walking around on the streets get their designer originals, anyway?"

Mark bowed gallantly and gestured her to precede him through the door of the small boutique near which they were standing. Meredith's heart gave a funny little catch when he did that, and she smothered a smile. *Where is your tricornered hat and your prancing black stallion, milord?*

Mark surprised her by taking an interest in her browsing. The young salesclerk gave them the customary welcoming smile, and Mark spoke to her as though he knew her. But Mark had spoken to everyone they passed that way that day. The small-town atmosphere was still pervasive. For not the first time Meredith wondered which of these fresh-scrubbed, conservatively dressed, undeniably plain and very young women Mark Brasfield found appealing. Which ones did he date? Whom did he share his bed with when the occasion arose? Was there a single woman in this town who could provide a match for his singular good looks, his incisive wit, his effusive personality? Or did he settle for second best? Perhaps he had a girlfriend out of town somewhere whom he visited occasionally. Perhaps he got his kicks out of conducting clandestine affairs with the under-twenty-five set. The curiosity was becoming almost an obsession with Merry.

"There certainly are a lot of young people here," she commented innocently when she could stand it no longer.

"New industry always attracts young talent," Mark responded, and shook his head over a blue-and-white polka-dot sheath she had picked up.

Meredith replaced the sheath and flipped idly through the rack. "You seem to know almost everyone in town," she said, probing a little harder.

"I get around." He pulled out a white cotton dress with a shirred bodice and a deep ruffle at the hem, holding it up inquiringly.

Meredith shook her head, grimacing. "I'd look like an albino hippopotamus in that."

Mark's eyes sparked mirth, but his smile was gently puzzled as he replaced the dress. "You really don't think you're very attractive, do you?" His tone implied that the concept was difficult for him to understand.

Meredith moved on to another rack, mostly to hide the sudden awkwardness she felt with his question. She lifted her shoulders negligently. "I don't think about it much at all."

"Why not?" he pursued.

Again she shrugged. "When you're seventeen and the most complimentary thing you've ever been called is 'Amazon,' you tend to stop thinking in terms of being attractive and settle for merely 'presentable.'" And she scowled in vague annoyance. How had the conversation gotten turned around to her? "We were talking about you," she reminded him.

"Me?" Mark leaned gracefully against the dress rack, his elbow propped on the top of it, his knuckles resting against the corner of his mouth. "I could never wear any of this stuff," he confided blandly, gesturing. "Don't have the legs for it."

Meredith flashed him a quick look of appreciative humor, and his eyes softened. He seemed to be studying her very peculiarly.

Meredith turned quickly back to the dresses. "I was saying," she put forth casually, "that you seem to know most of the young ladies in town."

It had come out most ungracefully, and Merry was sure that if she glanced at him, those light eyes would be dancing madly. So she deliberately did not. She felt color creep up the back of her neck from the force of his laughing gaze, and she flipped all the way to the size nines, furious with herself.

"And you are wondering," Mark helped her out easily, "which ones of them I know, er, better than I know the others."

There was no mistaking the unabashed amusement in his tone, and Merry did not look up. "I believe I told you," he answered, anyway, "that the social life in this town is very dull." And his voice softened a fraction. "Or at least it was until now."

Meredith swallowed back her embarrassment and made herself return to her own dress size, concentrating this time on the selection. Well, that answered that—more or less, anyway. Or perhaps not at all. With rising irritation, she realized she had succeeded in doing nothing except let him know that she was interested in the details of his "social" life and left herself open to an invitation to improve it. *Dumb, Merry. Really dumb.*

"You never considered the advantages of being an Amazon?" he inquired just when she had thought the subject was dropped.

Meredith looked up, surprised by the gentle alertness with which he was watching her, and she gave what she hoped was a casual, dismissive laugh. "Like being able to reach the top shelf in the kitchen without a step stool or beat all my dates at tennis or being invited to play quarterback for the minor league football team? Sure, all the time."

"No." Before Meredith was even aware of what he was doing, Mark had stepped in front of her, very close, and brought his hands to rest on her hips.

Meredith lost her breath as, with a gently increasing pressure of his fingers, Mark brought her against him, strong thighs against thighs, abdomens touching, her pelvis cradled firmly and neatly into his. "Like this," he said softly. His eyes were a melting pot of shadow and light, his breath a butterfly whisper against her cheek. Merry could feel her heart leap into action, and its source seemed to be the place where her body curved into his, his thumbs caressed her hipbones and his fingers pressed their individual brands into her flesh. "See how well we fit together?" he suggested huskily. "Perfect match."

It might have been twenty seconds, it might have been much less, that Meredith was caught within his spell, his eyes and his curving half smile stroking their explicit message into her brain like curious, insistent fingers. Opening up her secrets, garnering her response, filtering his desire into every pliant cell of her body. She could no more shield from him the answering awareness that leaped to her wide, startled eyes than she could prevent the flush that was creeping over her skin or the erratic skipping of her heart or the tightening of her lungs, which only this moment seemed to be breathing again. *Yes,* she thought. *We fit well together.*

Meredith stepped away abruptly and blindly pulled a dress from the rack. "I think I'll try this one," she blurted out, and turned swiftly to make her escape.

Mark calmly took the dress from her and replaced it with another from the rack. He was still watching her with that tender, half-amused smile. "Try this one," he suggested.

Meredith accepted it without question and darted into the fitting room.

She took a moment to press her hands over her hot cheeks in the privacy of the curtained cubicle. In a public place, already! Right between the size fives and the size twelves, within perfect range of the bland-faced saleswoman and the robotic smiles of curious customers. If he could do that to her in broad daylight in a busy little dress shop, what would happen if they were alone, in candlelight, with wine and a nearby sofa or bed...?

You'll melt all over him, Merry. You knew that from the first minute you saw him, didn't you? And now he knows it, too.

So what? she decided, and pulled her sweater over her head with a swift and irritated motion. He was probably used to it. A man like Mark probably had his choice of any sweet young thing in town; it would be no big surprise that a tall blond stranger should turn to jelly at his touch. He was used to trying out his charm and used to getting the response he wanted. He would hardly be impressed by Meredith Griffin's breathless adoration.

Okay, she told herself firmly, stepping out of her jeans. *You can be just as sophisticated as he is. So it's not every day of your life that a man right off the cover of a book walks into your life. So it's not every day that a stranger touches you and turns your bones to mush. He doesn't have to know that. No big deal.*

She told herself that, but she did not for one minute believe she would be able to carry it off.

The dress Mark had chosen was not only a perfect fit but the perfect style. For some reason that irritated Merry. The dress was a sleeveless black cotton blend with a slightly scooped neck, low

waist and gathered skirt. The hem was decorated
with a row of vibrant red, yellow and blue piping,
and the jacket had three-quarter-length sleeves
that were trimmed with narrower rows of the
same piping. The black brought out the sheen of
her hair and the color of her cheeks, the style flat-
tered her figure, and the contrast of bright trim
added an aura of casual festivity to the entire effect. This was one dress she could wear without
feeling like a fool, and she had to admit reluctantly that among all his other virtues the man had
impeccable taste.

Meredith did not model the dress for Mark but
dressed quickly in her jeans and sweater and came
out of the fitting room with her face composed
and her stride cheerful. No big deal, she told herself, smiling brightly at Mark. Over and forgotten.
And inside a treacherous little voice mocked,
Liar.

"What did you think?" Mark inquired. He was
either taking his cue from Merry, or the episode
had really not been anything out of the ordinary
for him. His smile was easy, his manner light, and
nothing in the way he looked at her suggested he
was even aware that less than ten minutes earlier
she had been ready to swoon at his feet with all
the dramatic flair of an old-time romantic heroine.

"Perfect fit," she responded, and made her
way to the cash register. "You're very patient.
Most men hate going shopping with women."

A quirk of self-mockery deepened the line near
his lips. "That's the second time," he pointed out,
"that you've used that phrase—'most men.'"

Don't you think you've known me long enough to realize I'm not like 'most men'?"

"Ah, the eternal male ego," she retorted. "Always indignant at the thought of being merely average."

His eyes laughed with a subtle confidence that needed no reassurance from her answer. "And am I?" he insisted. "Am I merely average?"

Meredith looked at him for a moment, a dry smile disguising the truth that he so obviously already knew. "Only in the sense," she replied, "that like in *most men*—" she emphasized the phrase with a deliberate lift of her brows "—your ego requires constant stroking."

He laughed and touched her arm lightly to guide her around a panty-hose display in the center aisle.

"Besides," Meredith added as the salesclerk smilingly handed her the package and wished them both a very pleasant afternoon, "I haven't known you very long at all—less than twenty-four hours, to be exact—and I don't know anything about you at all. How can I tell what you're like or not like?"

"Intuition?" he suggested, and they stepped out into the sunlight again.

That, of course, was no reply at all, and just as Meredith was about to point that fact out, Mark suggested easily, "How about an early lunch? We can take sandwiches to the park."

So he didn't like to talk about himself. An admirable characteristic in a man, all things considered. It was not his fault that Meredith had a burning desire to know everything about him, and who but a complete fool would want to blurt out his life's story to a stranger after less than twenty-four hours' acquaintance. *You did, Merry.* The sneaking little admission came to mock her. He knew absolutely everything there was worth knowing about her before dinner was over the night before. That made her feel disadvantaged, cheated somehow. She resolved to find out more about this man, whatever the cost. She refused to admit that the real reason behind her obsessive curiosity was mainly to fuel her daydreams in the weeks to come, when she had gone back home and the memories of him were all she had left.

They stopped by a café that featured things like alfalfa sprouts sandwiches and yogurt milk shakes—the town seemed to be very big on health foods—and ordered lunch to go. "So," invited Meredith casually as they left the shop for the spring morning again, "how long have you lived here?"

"A couple of years." Mark put his hand protectively on her elbow as they crossed the street.

"What made you decide to leave Wall Street?"

"Boredom, ulcers and a total lack of ambition."

"What kind of work do you do now?"

"Financial management. Do I get to read this story in the evening paper?"

Meredith acknowledged the teasing glint in his eye with one calmly raised eyebrow. "Unfortunately," she replied pointedly, "not all of us are blessed with your amazing gift of insight. Some of us have to be more direct if we want information."

The quirk of his lips was enigmatic. "So that's what we're doing," he murmured. "Gathering information." His fingers brushed her back, and he gestured toward a budding elm tree a few yards away. "Let's sit over there."

Meredith sank to the springy new grass and accepted the yogurt shake and sandwich he passed to her. Merry did not know what was inside the sandwich except a great deal of it was green, and she was beginning to understand how Mark kept so slim and fit. "Tell me more about Kevin," he invited, not giving her a chance to resume her interrogation. "How did he get involved with the Source of Enlightenment, anyway? How can you be sure he's here?"

Meredith opened her mouth to reply, and then her lips tightened in a dry acknowledgment of his distraction techniques. "You really don't like to talk about yourself, do you?" she challenged gently.

He was busy unpacking the remainder of their lunch from the white paper bag, and Merry could not see his eyes. "Only because I find myself so incredibly boring." He tore open a waxed paper sack of something that looked like small orange potato chips and set it on the grass between them. "Carrot chips," he explained. "They're not half bad."

Merry took up a chip and munched on it thoughtfully, watching him. It was the perfect setting for him. The sunshine did magnificent things to his eyes and painted deep streaks of red in his hair. The lacy shadows from the tree beneath which they sat cast waving patterns of light and dark over his face, hiding parts of his countenance, highlighting others, making his expression completely impossible to catch. His long body was relaxed and graceful in a half-lounging posture upon the grass, the soft colors of springtime the ideal backdrop for his rugged beauty. Around them, young mothers pushed strollers, old men read the paper on stone benches, and a few couples had lunch beneath the trees just as they were doing. He was a part of the scene, yet separate from it. Blending into the atmosphere, yet giving it distinction. As different from all that surrounded him as a three-dimensional character in a one-dimensional photograph.

"I think," observed Meredith slowly, "that it's because you're afraid of letting anyone too close."

He laughed, quickly and automatically, but not before Meredith caught a flicker of uneasiness begin to cross his eyes. That was the first sign of vulnerability she had seen in him, and the sensation of recognition that flowed through her was warm and enveloping. So he was real, after all. Not just the product of some artist's imagination but a living person with flaws and weaknesses. It was comfortable knowledge, and Meredith wished she could tell him so. But she had the distinct impression that any such confession would only serve to make Mark uncomfortable.

"Okay, you win," he said, and he gave every impression of being completely at ease as he tore off a corner of his sandwich and popped it into his mouth. "My life's story is yours for the asking. What do you want to know?"

She was hardly likely to receive a better invitation than that, and Merry accepted it enthusiastically. "At least," she retorted, "as much as you know about me. Start at the beginning."

"Born and educated in Hartford, Connecticut," he recited by rote. "Product of a workaholic and overbearing father and mother with a martyr complex, neither of whom had much interest in raising a child. No siblings, fortunately for all concerned; I lettered in track in high school and majored in business administration at Harvard, joined the brokerage firm of Waterman and Winslow at age twenty-three and progressed from there upward to become one of the most ruthless tyrants on Wall Street. At age thirty, decided there must be a better way to make a living and accepted a very lucrative offer that brought me to Stonington, Kansas. Which is not to overlook a series of tawdry and ultimately meaningless love affairs over the years, including one living arrangement that lasted three months and two days—which was three months longer than necessary for both of us. I've never been married or even considered it, which is the legacy of a strife-ridden childhood, I suppose, and no—" now he looked at her, his eyes clear and straight and revealing absolutely nothing "—I don't like to let people get too close. Does that about cover it?"

His tone was mild and his expression at ease, but that was only a disguise for deeper emotions. Meredith felt something inside her soften toward him and reach for him, almost as though to offer comfort for the things he did not tell her. He gave no indication of bitterness, but it was there. He showed her no sign of secret pain, but she could feel it. There was a vast void of things he would never tell her, yet rather than pushing her away, it seemed to draw her closer.

He was a man who was unaccustomed to sharing himself, that much was clear. He had never found anyone he could trust enough to open himself to, anyone he cared for enough to admit vulnerabilities, and so he remained alone. Perhaps someday he would find someone. And Meredith found herself wishing, suddenly and intensely, that that someone could be her.

Meredith took a bite of her sandwich and was surprised to find it was quite good. The bread was the same thick, rich brown bread they had the night before, the filling had a pungent, woodsy taste with the definite flavor of hazelnuts and cream cheese. Meredith watched him while she ate, and he met her gaze openly and without reserve, enjoying his own sandwich. Finally, Meredith decided, "That's a pretty sketchy outline for a life, if you ask me."

"That's because I only hit the highlights." He sat up to reach for his own shake.

"Sure you didn't leave out anything important?"

As he sat up, the distance that had been between them was closed by several feet. Now their shoulders almost brushed, and he was so close she could catch the hint of subtly expensive cologne; when he looked at her, their faces were mere inches apart. Meredith saw that roguish line of self-mockery at his lips deepen, and the misty softening of his eyes made her heart jerk and then flutter, warning her of what he was about to do before he did it.

"One or two details," he admitted, and he reached out and took a strand of her hair between his fingers. His eyes followed the movement, and the delicate way he separated the golden strands, the quiet, almost worshipful absorption with which he studied the wires of yellow-and-white light that played through them, caused a strange alteration in the pace of Merry's breathing. His tone was very serious, but his voice husky. "Like the fact," he said, bringing his eyes back to hers with a sober frankness that looked almost like a warning, but a warning Merry was in no frame of mind to take, "that I cheat at solitaire and deliberately put tin cans in with paper items on trash day. That my whole life has been sold to the highest bidder and I have a despicable tendency to follow the course of least resistance. And like the fact that I am extremely attracted to you and right now the course of least resistance seems to be to kiss you. Do you mind?"

Every ounce of awareness within Merry seemed to be concentrated, like electricity traveling along a conducting wire, on the point where Mark's thumb touched the corner of her lips, massaging with a gentle, almost infinitesimal circular motion, then moving a fraction to brush the smooth undercurve—and on his eyes, alert and waiting, yet shaded with a lazy, sensual fog that hid a multitude of inviting, intriguing and ultimately fascination messages. *No, I don't mind at all,* Meredith thought helplessly, and she could hardly hear the sound of her breathing anymore.

Yes it was the sound of her own voice, tight and odd-sounding and a little unsteady, that broke the spell between them. 'H-here?'' she said.

Slowly, like water droplets trailing off a waxy leaf, the magnetic absorption that bound Mark to her began to disperse, leaving Merry disappointed and confused and regretful. Why had she said that? In other circumstances a kiss in a public park would seem the most natural thing in the world. In other circumstances thoughts of her environment would have been the last thing to intrude upon a magic as powerful and as exclusive as that which had existed briefly between her and Mark. But somehow it was not like other circumstances. The park was not like any other, and the thought of all those conservatively dressed, blandly smiling men and women witnessing their tenderness or their passion had the power to distract Merry, to intimidate her and bring her with a jolt back to the point of caution. Something about the atmosphere seemed to throb with disapproval, and even though it frustrated and confused her, Merry knew she could not kiss Mark there, in full view of all those prying eyes. And worse, Mark seemed to know it, too.

His hand dropped slowly from her face, his lips formed a slow, regretful smile, and the tenderness in his eyes faded to cynicism. "Public interaction between members of the opposite sex," he admitted dryly, moving away, "is not against the law here—just frowned upon. And of course," he added lightly, picking up his yogurt shake, "the last thing you need is to be branded a scarlet woman."

Meredith frowned into the strawberry depths of her own shake, watching the swirling patterns she made with her straw while trying to regain a normal speaking tone and the usual rhythm of her breathing. She felt cheated, deprived and a little angry. What was it with this crazy town, anyway? And why would a man like Mark Brasfield choose to live his life in a time bubble that was sixty years removed from the rest of the world?

A voice above her shoulder made her jump, reinforcing that uneasy feeling that they were being spied upon. "Good afternoon," it said, and Mark smiled a welcome in the direction of the intruder.

"This is someone you need to meet, Merry," Mark said, and Meredith twisted around with an automatic smile to face the man above her.

He was not as young as the others, perhaps close to Mark's age, but the cropped hair, blank smile and white uniform of the Source of Enlightenment sent an automatic shudder of revulsion through her that Merry tried to keep out of her eyes. *Paranoia,* she scolded herself. *He hasn't really been watching you all this time, ready to interrupt when it looked as though things were getting too intimate. That really isn't coldness you see in his eyes, just blankness. That's not suspicion you feel from him, just curiosity. You're overreacting, as usual.*

"Meredith Griffin," Mark introduced, "this is

Brother Chi." The slight, almost unnoticeable
quirk of his eyebrow was a rueful apology for the
strange appellation. "He lives at the temple,"
Mark added. "Maybe he knows your brother.
Merry is here to visit her brother," Mark explained to Brother Chi, and there was no sign of
reaction whatsoever on the other man's face.
"His name is Kevin."

Brother Chi looked down at her, his smile in
place, his face as blank as the shadow of the
moon. But there was something in his eyes, a
flicker of something so brief and so vague that
Merry thought she might have imagined it—
something that could have been distaste or defen-
siveness or even a warning. And it was gone so
quickly that Meredith could grasp nothing more
than the slight shiver the thought of it sent down
her spine.

"Peace upon you, sister," he said smoothly,
ever smiling. "We are all brothers under the
Great Father."

Mark shot her a wry look of amused understanding, and that, combined with Meredith's
own irritation with the condescending nonsense
that had just issued forth from the mouth of a
man who looked old enough to know better, forti-
fied her into a frank response. "Does that mean,"
she enquired of Chi coolly, "that you don't know
a boy by the name of Kevin or simply that you
won't tell me?"

Of course nothing about the man's face changed.
It did not grow harder; the eyes were not really
colder. If anything, the tranquil smile only deep-

ened. "Please come and commune with us at the temple anytime," he invited. "All your brothers and sisters in the truth will welcome you." And he turned to include Mark in his benevolent departing smile. "Peace be upon you both."

Meredith tried to subdue the sinister little shiver that once again attacked her spine as he left. *You're being narrow-minded, Merry. The guy's got a right to his own beliefs.* And another part of her mind shot back indignantly, *The guy's a nut! Did you see the way he looked at you? Like he could bring a knife up square between your ribs and never blink an eye, never stop smiling.*

You're exaggerating, Merry. Paranoia again.

But in the end she could not help murmuring, rubbing her arms against the sudden coolness of the shaded breeze, "Is he for real?"

Mark's smile was both sympathetic and amused. "I'm afraid so. They're harmless enough," he assured her. "They just take a little getting used to. Don't look so worried."

But Meredith couldn't help being worried. She couldn't help thinking about Kevin, under the control of these people, acting like these people, thinking like them. Did they think at all? Would there be anything that was the bright, quickwitted Kevin remaining behind the implacable mask of inner contentment? Would she even know him? Or worse, would he know her?

Following the progress of her thoughts with the increasing shadows of despair on her face, Mark reached over and gently covered her hand with his. "It'll be okay," he said quietly, convincingly.

"You'll find your brother, I promise. Cheer up, okay?"

The tender, persuasive upturn of his lips coaxed a smile from her, and she nodded. The way his forefinger stroked the back of her hand was a soothing, hypnotic pleasure, and sitting there with him in the spring sunshine, looking into those gentle, smiling eyes, she found it easy to forget the less wonderful things about life. It was easy to forget anything that was not peaceful and pleasant and watercolor-pure; it was almost too easy to forget what had brought her there.

And, of course, there was danger in that.

Reluctantly, she withdrew her hand. "I'm sorry to involve you in my problems," she said, smiling a little uncertainly. "It's nice of you to try to help."

His smile was easy and relaxed. "I'm the only friend you've got in town," he reminded her. "And what are friends for?"

Merry laughed. She liked the sound of that. "To friends," she said, lifting her cup to him.

"Even those who cheat at solitaire and refuse to separate their trash?" he inquired.

"Beggars can't be choosers," she retorted, and their cups touched in a toast.

The sparkling moment of shared smiles, teasing, and relaxed gazes was warm and intimate, and Merry felt the pleasure of it seep all the way into her bones. The laughter on her face grew quieter, and she felt compelled to say simply, "Thanks, Mark."

He raised his eyebrows. "For what?"

"For being such a nice man."

For just a second there was a flicker of surprise in his eyes that seemed to be mixed with a quick flash of denial, but he only smiled easily and got to his feet. "You may have cause to retract that statement at a later date," he returned lightly, and began to gather up their wrappings. He deposited them in a gaily painted buttercup-yellow trash can, and Meredith got to her feet, brushing the grass off her jeans. Mark glanced at his watch. "It's a quarter after one," he said. "Will thirty minutes give you enough time to change? I'll meet you in the lobby a little before two, if that's okay."

Meredith picked up her package and said, frowning a little, "I hate for you to hang around town waiting for me for almost an hour. I can hurry."

"No problem," he assured her. "I've got to pick up a few groceries and run the car through the car wash. Take your time."

Somehow it felt awkward to end the growing sense of intimacy that had been between them since they entered the park on such a casual, impersonal note. But perhaps that was the way he wanted it. Intimacy was not within his repertoire, and his smooth changes of mood were no more than his method of protecting himself. Meredith had to honor that, no matter how much she wished it could be different, and she gave him a bright, if somewhat false, smile as she turned to go.

"Merry," he called after her softly, and she

turned. His smile was tender. "It's going to be all right," he promised.

Merry believed in that moment that it would.

THE MAN AT THE DESK tipped open a folder, and half a dozen black-and-white photographs came spilling out. Some were blurred, signifying the use of a telescopic lens; some were admirably sharp. All of them were of the same woman— tall, blond and aggressive-looking, dressed in jeans, a cowl-necked sweater and a paisley headband. She laughed, she walked, she rested under the shade of a tree, she smiled over a cup of coffee. Reverend Abraham Samuels studied them with no more than a cursory interest.

At length, he opened another file. "So this is the brother?" he grunted, glancing through it absently.

The man he addressed crossed the room and worked the combination on a safe that was neatly concealed behind the false back of a credenza. "Do you want some?" he offered lifting out a bottle of scotch.

Samuels glanced up, shook his head and leaned back in his chair, lifting his feet to his desk and crossing them at the ankles. "So what's the problem?" he demanded. "She just wants to see the boy, right?"

Samuels was a big man, towering six-feet-five without any props; the flowing white robes, piercing dark eyes and booming voice commanded respect in any crowd and accounted for at least half of his enormous sway over an audience. But in his own office, with his trusted advisers, intimidation techniques were superfluous and a waste of energy. The man who calmly poured himself a drink and went to sit in the shadows of the open window again knew exactly what was required of him, exactly how far he could go. A cynical, partially disinterested smile curved his lips as he replied, "Meredith Griffin is one determined young lady. I wouldn't underestimate her if I were you. She could be trouble."

"Hell, aren't they all?" Samuels chuckled and ran a hand over his completely bald head. He tapped a cigarette from the pack on his desk and lit it with a flick of his finger, shrugging. "So let her see the kid. We've got nothing to worry about with him; he's wrapped up tight. She'll give up and go home."

"I'm not so sure I'm in any rush to see her do that," the other man remarked absently.

For a moment Samuels's shrewd dark eyes quickened with warning and even a measure of concern, then he laughed, scattering ashes along the polished desk top with a careless flick of his wrist. "You keep your women to your own time, friend," he advised. "This is business."

A faint smile hovered around the lips of the man in the shadows. The subdued gleam in his eyes was as cool and calculating as any Samuels could have wished for. "So it is," he agreed mildly.

With suddenly alerted interest, Samuels inquired, "Do you have some . . . special plans for her?"

The only reply was a shrug and an enigmatic "Perhaps."

Samuels studied him for another moment. One of his most trusted advisers, a man with a level head on his shoulders if ever there was one. He had never doubted him and had never had cause to. The man was motivated by only one thing—greed. And that was the only kind of man Samuels would trust.

He could keep secrets, Samuels decided, play his games. He had nothing to worry about.

"All right." Samuels swept the photographs into his desk drawer and tapped ashes into a sacramental incense burner, brisk and businesslike. "Let's see what you've got on Astra."

But as the man in the shadows moved to open his briefcase, Samuels looked up again, his eyes narrowed with thoughtfulness. He had to give just one last caution. "You just make sure you keep your girlfriend in line," he said. "We're too damn close now to let some snooping female foul up the works. I'm holding you responsible," he said, piercing the other man with his gaze. "Get her in and out of here as fast as you can. The last thing we need is—" and his eyes fastened meaningfully on the other man "—complication."

The man's smile was the perfect complement for the gold emblem he wore on his tunic, as smooth and as confident as any ever seen outside this inner sanctum. "I promise," he said quietly. "No complications."

Chapter Five

The first thing Meredith noticed when she opened the door to her room was the faint but definite odor of alcohol. It did not take her long to trace the source to an upturned bottle of vodka in her trash can. She bent down to pick it up; it was empty. "Son of a...!" The soft exclamation trailed off into impotent anger as she let the empty bottle drop with a thud back into the plastic trash can.

Secret lushes on the housekeeping staff? She doubted it very seriously. More likely some self-righteous, doctrine-spouting militant had poured the entire contents down the sink, thus accounting for the odor. Her brows lowered ominously, and smoothing her hands purposefully on her hips, Merry straightened up and marched toward the bathroom to confirm her suspicions. How dare they! Who the hell did they think they were, anyway? This was her room, her vodka, and what right did they have to invade her privacy and destroy her property?

She angrily flipped on the light in the dressing room, and there she stopped.

The contents of Merry's cosmetics case were arranged neatly on the vanity just as she had left them. Toothbrush, mouthwash, hairbrush, nail polish, all in order. And glaring down at her from the wide mirror, scrawled in garish coral lipstick, were the words: Get Out While You Still Can.

Meredith stared at them for a long time.

She stared at them, and she felt a slow creeping sensation of icy revulsion stealing into her veins as the graphic nature of the warning burned itself into her mind. It was so ugly. It was so hateful and pointed that someone should have entered her room, violated her domain and left this brutal warning to haunt her. Merry felt hunted down, vulnerable, helpless and terrified. Who would want to do this to her? Why would anyone want to frighten her? What had she done to anyone here? Why did they hate her so? Why?

They had used her lipstick. Somehow this, above all else, seemed to be the final indignity. Merry's hand was not quite steady as she reached for the coral tube and pulled off the lid. When she saw the smeared, flattened remnants of the lipstick, a sudden burning sensation flooded her eyes, and she let the metal tube clatter onto the counter as she choked back a sob.

Merry gripped the edge of the counter furiously, blinking back the weakness. No, damn it, this was what they wanted. They wanted to intimidate her, to violate her, and she would not let some vicious vandal with the imagination of a six-year-old get the better of her. Why? God only knew. These people were crazy. The whole damn town was crazy. Maybe they didn't like her wearing slacks. She wore makeup and kept a secret bottle of vodka in her room; she did not belong there. Self-righteous vigilantes did not need a reason; they only needed an excuse.

Merry wet a towel and plied it with soap, then viciously began to erase the hateful scrawl from the mirror. Some stupid hick's idea of justice, that was all. She would not let it get to her.

But she was still frightened. And suddenly, very badly, she wanted Mark.

A HALF HOUR LATER, showered and changed, she went downstairs to meet Mark. The black dress had lost none of its appeal, though she was beginning to hate the reason for it. Because the temperature was warming up and because the dress really looked better without it, Merry did not wear the jacket. She carried it over her arm, though, just in case there was some rule about women not being allowed to show bare upper arms. She was beginning to catch on to the way these people thought. And deliberately, almost spitefully, she wore her most glamorous daytime makeup, even though she had to scrape the bottom of the tube with her finger to get enough lipstick to cover her lips. She looked fresh, sassy and very big-city. Approval lit Mark's eyes when he saw her.

"You look gorgeous," he told her, and he took both her hands in greeting. "Going to take the place by storm, are you?"

Merry's eyes narrowed determinedly, for even the thrill she felt in Mark's touch could not mitigate the slow, rolling anger that formed in her stomach whenever she thought about one of those bland smiling faces breaking into her room, desecrating her property. "If I have to," she assured him grimly.

A perceptive eyebrow shot up, and Mark turned to lead her outside. "You seem a bit upset," he commented mildly.

The trauma of the incident had faded somewhat, and Merry was able to tell him in calm, concise tones what she had found when she returned to her room. She watched the slow darkening of Mark's features as she recited her tale, but he did not speak until they were both settled comfortably in his luxurious Buick. He seemed to be considering the matter as he started the ignition.

"Did you inform the hotel management?" he asked at last.

Merry rather shamefacedly admitted she had not. "I was so mad I washed the whole thing off, and then I felt foolish about calling the management to complain about a blurred mirror."

Mark shook his head disapprovingly. "It was obviously someone on the staff. They should be informed."

"About the theft of an illegal bottle of booze?" Meredith tried to laugh. "That's going to be little awkward, isn't it?"

Mark half lifted one shoulder as though in agreement. Then he sighed. "Merry," he said, his tone a mixture of apology and explanation, "this town is a town in transition, a mixture of the old and new, progress versus tradition. There's still an occasional flare of resentment or hostility, and sometimes an innocent bystander gets caught in the middle." He looked at her and smiled. "Try not to let it bother you, okay?"

Meredith did not understand what he meant about transition and hostility or why anyone would want to take their frustrations out on her. But when he looked at her that way, with the smile that began first in his eyes and spread its way down to his lips, softening his whole face and drawing her toward him, it did not matter. She would accept anything he said and be happy for it.

The drive to the temple took about twenty minutes. On the way out of town Mark pointed out the community of neat, beautifully landscaped condominiums where he lived, and Merry was struck by the fact that although the sandstone buildings were certainly very modern and economically structured, they seemed to lack the character one usually expected in a residential area. They were very much like the office buildings in town.

She listened absently as Mark called her attention to a large graded portion of land and explained the plans for a new food-processing plant there that would be a model in the field of energy conservation and pollution control. He went on to discuss the probability of the new interstate highway that would be required to handle all the traffic generated by the new jobs growing up around Stonington. And then he turned off onto a smaller road that was so new and well kept it looked like a driveway.

That, Merry was to discover, was more or less what it was. The road led nowhere except to an enormous set of iron gates set in a concrete arch. Sculpted into the concrete high overhead, was the elliptical symbol with the intertwining V's, and there was no other sign to announce that they had arrived.

A young man wearing the white tunic and perpetual smile that was the uniform of the place emerged from the gatehouse, and Mark gave him their names and the purpose of their visit. Merry felt tension coil within her stomach as the gates swung open and the car inched through. The metal clanging as the gates slammed behind them grated on her nerves.

"Don't expect to see your brother today," Mark warned her quite unnecessarily. "And don't expect any of the people you meet to be able to answer your questions. You'll have to follow the proper procedure and not—" he shot her a glance that was only half amused "—make trouble."

Merry widened her eyes innocently. "Do I look like a troublemaker?"

Mark's laugh was soft and relaxed, and it had a peculiar tickly effect just beneath Merry's breastbone. "That," he responded, "is only one of the things I like about you."

They were driving through a parklike area that, under other circumstances, would have been a pleasure to behold. Mark pointed out various experimental plants and shrubs that were being grown there and told her that it was one of the most advanced horticultural research facilities in the world. There were artfully landscaped flower beds and charming bridges over clear-water streams, and everywhere she looked men and women in white tunics were wandering around, working in the vineyards, driving lawn tractors, tilling the flower beds, pruning the shrubs. And Merry couldn't help it. She had to search every face.

"How many people live here?" she asked at last in a small voice. They had been driving five minutes, and she had yet to see the first building. The vastness of the place was beginning to overwhelm her.

"I'm not sure," Mark replied. "A lot."

The man had a gift for understatement. To operate a facility this size must take hundreds. Perhaps even thousands.

"Everyone has a job here," he did volunteer, though, "assigned by his or her own specialty or talent. A lot of the people who live here were professionals in their—" his voice dropped wryly "—'other life.' Doctors, lawyers, accountants, teachers—and they do much the same here as they did before. The compound is completely self-sustaining. They even have their own fully equipped hospital here."

A fully equipped, completely self-sustaining community of robots. Meredith found the whole thing very eerie.

At last, Mark turned onto a gravel drive lined with neat low shrubs, and Meredith could see just beyond the curve the welcome signs of civilization—if civilization was a word that could ever be

accurately applied to the place. The first building
that came into view was long and flat and looked
as though it were fashioned from pink marble.
The roof was gabled with skylights, but there were
no windows. In front of it was a tall fountain
whose centerpiece was again that perpetual, elliptical symbol. Meredith was beginning to hate the
sign.

The main building spread outward, connecting
with other, smaller ones, interlocking to the side
and the back by covered walkways to several long,
low structures of the same marble structure that
looked like dormitories. She wondered if that was
what they were.

"Just get that thought out of your head," Mark
warned her when she voiced her speculation out
loud. "You are allowed to tour the temple and the
grounds, but that's all. These people are very
picky about what they call their 'inner space.'
There's no way you can get into the living quarters."

We'll just see about that, Merry thought, but she
smiled complacently at Mark and nodded agreement.

There were other cars in the parking area besides theirs and other people dressed in street
clothes lingering outside the open door of the
structure or sitting on the benches that lined it.
That took away some of the sinister atmosphere
for Merry, and she tried to relax. She tried to remind herself to be open-minded. She tried to
make herself promise to do as Mark said and not
make any trouble. For one day she would play it

their way and go by their rules. But if they still refused to allow her access to her brother, well, then, she decided grimly, all rules would be off.

Mark took her up to a young lady in a calf-length white tunic and long, straight silvery-blond hair. There were three or four other people in street clothes gathered around her, all looking just as curious and just as out of place as Meredith felt. The young girl smiled at Mark and then at Merry and greeted her in a low, tranquilly mesmerizing voice, "Welcome, sister. I am Sister Peace, and it is my great delight to serve as your guide on your voyage to inner contentment." She swept her smile to include the others around them and raised her voice a little. "If you all gather round, we will begin."

Merry murmured in an aside to Mark, "Sister Peace? Give me a break! She sounds like the hostess of an opium den."

Mark grinned and squeezed her arm bracingly. "Mind your manners," he whispered back. Then, in a normal tone of voice, the mischievous grin notwithstanding, he added, "Now if you'll excuse me, I've had the two-dollar tour already. I'll go see what can be done about making an appointment with your brother. Don't get into any trouble," he warned lightly, and he was gone before Merry could protest or call after him.

Merry would have preferred to have gone with him. If he was going to try to do something about Kevin, she *should* have gone with him instead of wasting time with a tourist's-eye view of the establishment. But before she knew it, she was being swept along with the others down a long marble corridor to the sonorous tones of Sister Peace, and she decided rather reluctantly that Mark was probably right. Left to her own devices, she would most likely do nothing but cause trouble and possibly destroy any chance she ever had of seeing Kevin. Mark was accustomed to dealing with these people; he knew how to employ diplomacy and tact. Meredith would not have been able to conceal her contempt and her anger long enough to hold a decent conversation.

There was something very, very strange about the tour. Meredith would not be able afterward to put it into words, not even for Mark, and whenever she thought about it, she would be assailed again by irritation with her own inadequacy of expression. It was like walking into another world. It was another world. It was still and suspended and insulated from anything outside its walls; it was totally removed from anything Meredith had ever known before.

The marble corridors were thick with sound-absorbing greenery. Overhead, fed by the skylights, was a veritable garden of hanging plants of every description, thick and lush and beautiful. The walls were lined with potted plants and terraced plants that seemed to grow right from the moss that covered the marble; from floor to ceiling not an inch of anything that was not green and living could be seen. The air was thick with a heavy, energy-sapping humidity, and Merry was glad she had not worn her jacket. The light was diffuse and eerie, like a mist of indistinct color that was generated within the plants themselves, rather than merely reflected by them. It was like stepping into some great undersea cave.

It was silent. The occasional figures in white tunics who passed glided like ghosts on bare feet, smiling pleasantly to no one and everyone. The only sounds were those of the voice of their guide and the shuffling movements of those who followed her, and even those sounds seemed to be absorbed, surrealistic and distant, signifying nothing. There was no conversation among the participants in the tour. The voice of Sister Peace was the guiding light of reason that they followed blindly.

It might have been the humidity or the crazy light or the unreal stillness of the place, but the entire atmosphere was one of tranquillity, almost mindless contentment. The senses absorbed the gentle onslaught of surrounding beauty: the mind was lulled into quiescence. Merry could understand why people would want to live there. How easy it would be to just put the mind on hold and sink into unquestioning peace in such a place; no challenges, no decisions, everything carefully controlled by a simple routine, surrounded by beauty and tranquillity and gentle people. . . .

Sister Peace took them through the various rooms within the temple. The Starlight Room, where devotees meditated cross-legged on rush mats beneath a gentle blue light that seemed to possess in and of itself a cleansing, healing quality. The Crystal Room, in which tropical plants seemed to grow from crystal stalagmites and stalactites and reflect an almost-blinding heavenly light toward the skylight in the roof. The Room of Divine Revelation. The Room of Inner Discovery. The Room of Self-contemplation. Each one with a mood of its own, each one more powerfully compelling and sensually hypnotic than the one before.

Sister Peace told them of the philosophy and guidelines of the Source of Enlightenment. The body was a temple. They did not eat red meat, imbibe alcohol, smoke cigarettes or consume sugar, all of which practices were anathema to the teachings of their earthly father, Reverend Samuels. They did not mark their faces with cosmetics or adorn their bodies with frivolous garments. They lived in complete harmony with nature. They disciplined their minds from earthly pleasures. They devoted their lives and the fruits of their labor to the church, which would one day lead the entire world to a discovery of the only truth.

Within the temple, she informed them, was a library that was open to the public six hours a day during the week. And now, if they would please follow her . . .

Meredith, lingering at the back of the group, turned the corner to follow, and as she did, her shoulder bumped that of another one of the white-shrouded devotees they had occasionally passed during the course of the tour, a dark-haired, extremely young woman who was moving in the opposite direction. Meredith turned with an apology, expecting to face no more than the senseless smile and slight inclination of the head that was the customary greeting of everyone who wore the uniform of the Source of Enlightenment.

But this young woman was not smiling. Her face was pale and her eyes red-rimmed, and when the small collision occurred, she had actually flinched backward, her eyes filling with quick and unmistakable fear.

And Meredith was jolted out of the apathy that had descended upon her since entering the place. Like a shattering of finely spun glass, the spell woven upon her by the pulsing silence, the cocoonlike atmosphere, the sonorous voice of Sister Peace, cracked and dispersed, leaving her clear-eyed and alert. It was not a haven for untroubled souls. The figures who walked the corridors were not robots with plastic smiles and programmed words. They were real people with thoughts and emotions and personalities of their own, real people who had been subjected to some subtle form of identity alteration, and this one was obviously very disturbed.

Meredith touched her arm lightly; the other woman pulled back. "Don't touch me!" she whispered in genuine alarm. "Don't let them see you talking to me!"

She tried to move past Merry, her eyes darting about in fear of discovery, but Meredith could not let her pass. She blocked the young woman's way, her heart thumping loudly. She could not get the picture of Kevin out of her mind; Kevin, confused and afraid, Kevin, with only a stranger to talk to. "What is it?" Meredith demanded softly. "What's wrong?"

The woman shook her head frantically, her eyes pleading. "If they see me like this, talking to you ... If they see I've been crying ..."

"What?" insisted Merry. "What will they do to you? Why were you crying?"

"They won't let me leave here!" The whisper was so soft it could hardly be distinguished, but the despair that backed it was loud and agonizing. "I thought it would be good, but it's not. I thought it was what I wanted, and I've asked them to let me go home, and they won't...." Her eyes filled with a mixture of horror and self-reproach as she realized the betrayal she had just spoken, and for a moment there was a horrible struggle on the woman-child's face. Meredith was certain for a second that she was going to turn and run.

"Let me help," Merry volunteered quickly, almost desperately.

Decision came into the young woman's face with a measure of desperate hope. "My name is Holly," she whispered. "My parents—"

"Ah, there you are, sister." Sister Peace approached Meredith at a gliding, smiling pace, her hand extended. "We thought we had lost you. Do come see our library. I think you'll find it most fascinating."

Sister Peace's hand fell lightly upon Meredith's arm, and it was the touch a nurse might give a patient or one a guard would give an inmate. Meredith found it suddenly repulsive, and she shrugged it off. The good sister did not appear to be offended but smilingly gestured the way.

When Meredith looked back quickly for the young woman named Holly, she was gone.

THE TOUR CONCLUDED by a circular route back in the airy marble foyer where it had begun. No other faces among those glimpsed on the return trip showed signs of desperation or despair. No eyes looked at her with pleading. Every face was a carbon of the other—serene, content, mindless. Meredith almost could have convinced herself she had imagined the episode with Holly, but she could not forget the hopelessness, the fear and the desperation that had emanated from that young woman. She was not there of her own free will, and Merry had not imagined that.

Merry jumped as a cool hand fell upon her shoulder. So insulated from the realm of reality had she been for the past hour that the touch of a human hand went straight to her nerve center. She whirled to face the tallest, most powerful-looking man she had ever seen.

He was shrouded in the flowing white robes of the church, the insignia of enlightenment gleaming goldenly on his chest. His head was shaved, and so was his face. He towered above Merry, and for the first time in her life she experienced the sensation of being small and insignificant. The man exuded an authority and a control that were palpable, though his dark eyes were kind and his smile complacent and welcoming. Merry knew without being told that it was the infamous Reverend Samuels.

"I hope you had a pleasant visit within our temple, sister," he said. His voice was deep and rolling, gentled now to a conversational tone. She could imagine that voice raising to enthrall millions, and those eyes...such an inner light in those eyes. Mesmerizing, captivating, like twin candle flames. "We are always happy to welcome those who come in search of the truth."

He spoke kindly; he smiled benevolently, wrapped in confidence and graciousness. Merry could see how easy it would be to trust him, to believe in his power, to follow his orders. She could understand how people of uncertain strength, desperately looking for a better life, could be drawn into the spell of the man and the place he had created. But he frightened Merry. Or perhaps it was anger. Since coming to his town, Merry was finding it increasingly difficult to differentiate between the two.

Her chin lifted defiantly, and she looked straight into those bottomless dark eyes. "The only thing I'm searching for," she told him evenly, "is my brother."

"Ah, yes." There was no alteration of the kind smile, and his head inclined graciously. "Your friend told me of it. We are always pleased when those from the outside show an interest in our work. I have spoken with your brother, and he will enjoy speaking with you on Monday."

Two things leaped to Meredith's consciousness immediately and competed with the joyous racing

of her heart for her attention. He had spoken to
Kevin. Kevin was alive and well, and this man had
spoken to him within the hour, had been close to
him, which meant that even now Kevin was
nearby, within touching distance, and she could
see him. But Monday. He had said Monday.
"Why not now?" she objected almost frantically.
"If he's here and you've talked to him, why can't
I see him now?"

Mark came up beside her and lay a quieting
hand on her arm, but she hardly felt it. The kind,
calm, ultimately benevolent expression of Reverend Samuels did not change. "You must understand, dear sister," he explained sympathetically,
"that the Guardians of the Truth lead a very sanc-
tified life. He must prepare himself for contact
with those from the outside. Though he is greatly
desirous that you should share in his contentment
and allow him to unfold the ways of enlightenment for you, he will spend the hours between
now and your return in meditation and—"

Merry exploded, "That's the biggest bunch of
bull—" and Mark's hand clamped down hard on
hers, choking off the word, and Merry's churning
wrath left her too breathless to continue.

The reverend's eyes softened with pity toward
the poor misguided soul who stood before him,
and Mark put in smoothly, "Thank you for your
time, reverend. Miss Griffin will be back Monday."

Reverend Samuels replied gently, "Peace be
upon you both," and glided away.

Meredith did not trust herself to speak until

they were out of the building. Kevin was there, trapped inside that insipid hothouse of mindless obedience, day by day sinking further into their mire. Kevin, fortifying himself against the contamination brought by his own sister. Kevin, wanting to show her the way to enlightenment. She felt ill.

The bright sunlight hit her like a cleansing jolt; the spring air was cool and refreshing after the cloying interior of the building. She took a deep breath, rubbing the flesh on her arms that had begun to prickle with the contrast in temperature, and she drank in the sights and sounds and smells around her greedily, hungrily. It was like waking from a nightmare. It was like being lost in the woods and suddenly stumbling upon home. Meredith had not realized what an eerie, disoriented feeling being inside that temple was until she stepped outside and the contrast of the real world hit her in the face like a slap. Grass that grew from the ground, not the walls. Birds chirping, breezes stirring. Automobiles, that great industrial symbol of modern civilization. Real people talking in real voices, wearing real clothes, smiling real smiles. It was all beautiful to her, and she felt weak with a wave of residual relief.

"Snake pit," she muttered, and slid into the front seat of the car as Mark opened the door for her.

Mark shot a glance of amused confusion as he prepared to close her door. "What?"

"The place is a snake pit," she repeated, and she was still rubbing her arms as though to rid herself of the sense of something sinister that clung to her like a sticky web. "Those people are certifiably over the edge. There should be a sign over the door that says, 'Abandon All Hope Ye Who Enter Here.'"

The amused puzzlement in Mark's eyes deepened a fraction. "Are you mixing your metaphors?"

Meredith did not think so. There was a method in the madness that permeated every corner of that sanctuary. Irrational behavior without cause was merely frenzy, but frenzy for a purpose was evil. And that was the word she had been searching for since the moment those metal gates had clanged shut behind them. Evil.

Mark slid behind the wheel of the car and started the engine, and Meredith leaned back against the seat and closed her eyes, trying to relax, trying to rid herself of the nightmarish quality of contamination the place had left upon her. The mindless faces, the hushed voices, the soporific heat, the artificial light... Credos repeated by rote, hypnotic smiles... And Kevin. Poor Kevin. Was he like Holly, desperately wanting to escape and terrified to try, or was he more like Sister Peace, his wonderful mind completely gone?

No. She could not think like that. If she started to think like that, she would go mad. She had to believe that there was something left of Kevin for her to reach, that he would still be her brother, that he had not been totally absorbed into that unthinking organism that promised fulfillment and delivered emptiness. She had to hope.

Merry released an unconscious breath of relief when they passed through the gates and put the clinging atmosphere of the place behind them. And until that moment, Mark did not speak, as though sensing she needed the time to compose herself.

"I thought you were going to blow it there for a minute," he commented mildly, glancing at her.

For a moment Meredith was confused; then her lips twisted downward dryly. "Oh. You mean with the good reverend." And of course Mark was right. He had gone to a great deal of trouble to arrange this for her, and she had almost spoiled it all by acting like a bad-tempered child. She must learn to control her volatile emotions better. Why couldn't she be as cool and calm as Mark? Why couldn't she learn to hide her feelings as well as he did?

"Thanks for rescuing me," she added. "I guess I got a little carried away."

Mark tilted his head in agreement, but the wry quirk of sympathy on his lips reassured her he was not upset with her. "Look, Merry," he said in a moment, "I know how you feel about your brother, and that has to be clouding your judgment somewhat, but don't you think you're overreacting to this whole thing a little? It's just a church, after all. Those people are no crazier than anyone else. People have a right to choose their own life-style—"

"No, they don't." Merry shook her head firmly, the anger and the horror beginning to knot in her stomach again. "It's wrong. They're preying on innocent victims. They're keeping people against their wills—"

Mark shot her a look of patent incredulity. "Now how do you presume to know that?"

Merry took an unsteady breath, forcing her hands to unclench. "There was a young woman in there," she told him. "Holly. She was terrified, Mark! She told me—she was afraid to even talk to me, but she told me she wanted to leave and they wouldn't let her. She was afraid of what would happen to her if she was even found talking to me! Does that sound like a person who has cheerfully chosen an 'alternative life-style' of her own free will?"

Merry saw with satisfaction the slight crease of concern appear between his brows. "No," he admitted. "It doesn't. So what did you do?"

"Nothing," Merry admitted helplessly, and she turned to look out the window again. "I think Holly was going to ask me to contact her parents, but then that Sister Peace person came back, and she ran away." She tilted her head back again and closed her eyes, trying to blot out the trapped desperation on the young woman's face. "It was pitiful, Mark," she said tightly. "When I think about Kevin..."

Mark reached over and took her hand. He said nothing, but simply held her hand, and she felt from him a strength and a reassurance that had the power to blot out all the horror that had gone before. For all the ugliness of the nightmare that had brought her there, Mark was the one wonderful thing that made it all almost worth it. She entwined her fingers with his and felt a swelling peace begin within her that slowly pushed other concerns into the background. Mark was there, and he was giving her courage. Nothing could be so bad as long as Mark was with her. She had only known him two days, but already she was becoming dependent on him—addicted, almost. She could hardly remember what her life was like before Mark, and she did not want to think what it would be like after.

Lost in her own slowly settling thoughts and the sensuous caressing motions of Mark's thumb against her palm, Meredith did not open her eyes until the car had stopped and the engine stilled. When she did, it was to see not the familiar façade of her own hotel but the small tidy lawn of a sandstone condominium.

"My place." Mark gently answered the question in her eyes, and he did not seem disturbed when Merry pulled her hand away.

Why was she surprised? This was what she had wanted wasn't it, on a deep and secret level, since they had said good night in the lobby the day before? To be alone with him, to get to know him, to be touched by him.

This is crazy, Merry. You've only known the man two days. You know perfectly well why he brought you here and what he expects once you get inside. This isn't like you, Merry. Not a bit.

She said, not quite meeting his eyes, "Mark, I really don't think— I mean, I think it might be better if you took me back to the hotel...."

He reached forward and gently grasped her

chin, turning her to face him. His smile was tender. "Let me guess," he said. "You're thinking that 'going to my place' is synonymous with going to bed. You're afraid if we spend any time at all alone together, we'll end up making love."

Meredith looked at him, clear-eyed and vulnerable, and even with so gentle a touch as his fingertips upon her chin, she could feel her pulse speed. "I think," she replied, more or less steadily, "it's a distinct possibility."

His smile deepened; his eyes softened with affection and understanding. "And I think," he replied, stroking her chin gently, "that we're both old enough to make that decision when the time comes." His hand moved away to trace the shape of her ear and then clasped the back of her neck, briefly and warmly, before leaving her.

"But right now," he said, moving away to reach for the door handle, "you're in need of a drink, some food and a sympathetic ear, not necessarily in that order. I'm happy to say I can offer all of the above." He paused before opening the door, and his eyes held nothing but the question and a promise to accept her answer without complaint. "What do you think?"

Merry did not hesitate very long. The horror of the afternoon was still too fresh, and the thought of going back to her isolated hotel room, haunted by the memory of a spiteful threat and a vigilante intrusion, filled her with revulsion. Even going back to town, where those white-shirted figures with their hateful gold emblem smiled at her from every corner, seemed almost more than she could bear. She did not want to be alone in the midst of a hostile environment. She needed a drink. She wanted to be with Mark.

And she smiled. "I think," she answered, "that's got to be the best offer I've had all day."

Chapter Six

Meredith hesitated a little at the door, and Mark's smile was both amused and beguiling. "Please come in," he invited graciously, and gestured her to precede him.

Meredith felt foolish for that brief moment of second thoughts. She was making far too big a deal out of this. Mark would think she had never been to a man's apartment before. Not that she exactly made a practice of it, but she certainly considered herself sophisticated enough to be beyond the first-date jitters. She tossed him a bright smile and stepped over the threshold.

The first thing that struck her was the air of almost breathtaking spaciousness; the second thing that struck her was the reason why: there was no furniture, or at least none to speak of. The wide, cathedral-ceilinged room was carpeted in stark white; the walls, of the same sheer white, formed an unbroken line of one-dimensional sameness that was a shock to the senses. The stark decor was broken first by a low octagonal table in the center of the room that held a single red tapered candle and by an A-shaped floor-to-ceiling window on the opposite wall through which uncurtained afternoon sunshine poured with dazzling brilliance. Upon the floor were scattered dozens of thick, comfortable-looking cushions of every conceivable shade, and Meredith's first cautious assessment was *Weird. Very weird.*

She came into the room warily, trying to keep her conservative middle-class tastes from showing. "Oriental?" she ventured, moving carefully around a grouping of cushions.

"Nope," replied Mark cheerfully, tossing his keys onto the glass-topped center table. "Redecorating. I'm always doing that; people tell me it's a sign of an unstable personality."

Meredith chuckled to herself and relaxed as Mark disappeared around a corner. She had had enough culture shock for one day; it was a relief to discover that his apparently eccentric tastes had a very natural, and very human, explanation. She did not think she could contend with a lecture on the mind-expanding virtues of Oriental sparsity that night.

Mark returned in a moment with a glass of Burgundy wine in each hand. "Sit down," he invited, handing Meredith her glass, "or lie down or stand up. Whichever looks most comfortable. Relax."

Meredith accepted the glass of wine and eyed the cushions skeptically. "It's a hard decision," she admitted.

Mark grinned and touched his glass to hers in a light salute. "Back in a minute," he said, and he paused at the exit to the hallway with a wink. "I'm just going to change into something more comfortable.''

Again Merry found herself chuckling to herself as she slipped off her shoes and lowered her long frame to a pile of orange and yellow cushions near the center table. She should have known to expect the unexpected from Mark. Nothing about the man was in keeping with the ordinary. Even his wine—she took an appreciative sip—was an unusual vintage, dusky, rich and potent. She was glad she had agreed to come there. She felt comfortable and welcome there, and already the tensions of the day were beginning to slip from her.

Mark came out of the bedroom in worn and faded jeans, a white sweat shirt and bare feet. His hair was bouncy and fluffy where it fell across his brow and curled at his neck, his step easy and light. He looked wonderful to her.

"Making yourself right at home, I see," he greeted her, moving her shoes under the table as he drew up a cushion and lowered himself to the floor beside her.

"How long have you lived like this?" she inquired on a stifled note of mirth.

"Not long." He shrugged, taking a sip of his wine. "A few days. The new furniture is being delivered next week, if the truck doesn't get bogged down in the mountains or trapped in spring floods. Just one of the disadvantages of living in the middle of nowhere."

She laughed. "Sounds like you have experience. So what are you redecorating it as?"

"High-tech. Lots of plastic and glass and those twisted pipe chairs that look like they belong in the cockpit of a space capsule."

Merry wrinkled her nose. "You'll hate it."

"Probably," he agreed. "I've hated everything else. What's your apartment like?"

"My mother calls it 'a potpourri of everyone else's tastes.' Early attic."

"Now that's one I haven't tried yet," he said, arranging another cushion behind his back and leaning back on his elbows.

"Quick, inexpensive and easy to come by," Merry assured him. "All you need is a handful of relatives with a lot of junk crowding up their garages."

"Well, that lets me out." His lashes shielded his eyes as he sipped from his glass again.

Meredith felt a twinge of sympathy for him. Worse than an orphan, he had grown up with parents who had not even cared enough for him to care for themselves or each other, with role models who taught him that the best way to handle a relationship was to either ignore it or be victimized by it. He had never known the loving closeness and quiet values imparted by her own family. But even that, Meredith realized with a pang of despair that made the wine taste sour in her throat, had not been enough to save Kevin. There was Mark, victim of a childhood of neglect, now happy and confident and independent, leading his own life; and there was Kevin, a boy with every childhood advantage, coupled by the support of a strong and loving family unit, now lost to the world and enmeshed in the mind-warping values of the search for true happiness. What made the difference? Where had they gone wrong?

Meredith blinked away the distressing train of thought and made a concentrated effort to distract herself. "Why do you stay here, Mark?" she asked. "I mean, it's obvious you don't belong here. You're so bright and polished and..."

She groped for the word, and Mark supplied with a wry twist of his brow, "Cosmopolitan?"

"Yes," Meredith conceded, her own lips tightening at one corner in dry amusement. "What has a place like this got to offer a man like you?"

Again Mark hid his eyes with his lashes as he glanced down at his glass. "Maybe," he suggested, "I'm not the kind of man you think I am."

And then, abruptly, before Merry could question or comment, he stood and placed his glass on the table. She watched as he crossed the room, slid back a panel of what appeared to be a completely seamless wall and pushed a button on the hidden stereo console. Soothing background music wafted through the room at a comfortable level.

Meredith arched her eyebrows appreciatively. "Sharp," she acknowledged. "What other little secret weapons do you have?"

"Well," he admitted modestly, closing the panel again, "if I hit that button over there by the light switch, the floor opens up and a king-sized bed rises to the surface. And there's a little switch under the cocktail table that causes a mirrored ceiling to appear, but other than that the place is pretty run-of-the-mill, I'm afraid."

"Just your average bachelor pad," she agreed soberly, and their eyes met for a comfortable moment of sparkling humor.

Mark sat beside her again, growing serious as he reached for his wine. "Merry," he said, "I really think you're approaching this whole thing with the wrong attitude. You can't come storming in here accusing these people of kidnapping and corrupting minors and who knows what else—you've got to be a little more open-minded. You've got to see it from their point of view. Sure, they're a little weird, but what's the harm?"

Merry watched him with steadily widening eyes and rapidly rising indignation, and the lovely mood between them was torn with an almost-audible sound. "What's the harm?" she repeated indignantly. "What's the harm?" He winced at her rising voice and her dangerously sparking eyes. "These kids are being *brainwashed*, that's the harm! They're being kept under that madman's spells against their will, forced to work for him, giving their *whole lives* to him for *nothing*! That's the harm!"

"Nobody's being brainwashed," Mark replied, and only a slight hint of impatience crept into his otherwise perfectly reasonable tone. "The place is a business, that's all, and like any other business they're selling a commodity for a price. What they're selling is contentment, happiness and security, and there are a lot of buyers out there,

Merry. All they're doing is giving the people what they want."

Merry stared at him, an awful, hollow feeling of utter confusion forming in her stomach. He did not understand. He did not understand at all. One moment she felt she knew him better than anyone she had ever known in her life, that she could trust him with anything, that a bond of understanding was forming between them that could surmount any obstacles, and the next she had to realize he was a stranger. He didn't understand at all.

"Mark," she said helplessly, "look at them! Look at the way they live, the way they act, the things they do! They're crazy! How can you defend them?"

"'Crazy' is a subjective judgment," he observed mildly, and leaned back on one elbow, his expression frank and unconcerned. "Besides, I'm not defending them. I'm really not interested enough in what goes on out there to defend or condemn them. It fascinates me a little, I guess, the way strict morality always does." And he shrugged, lifting his glass to his lips. "Perhaps because I have absolutely no morals of my own."

Her brows twisted into a puzzled, helpless frown. "Morality? Is that what you call it?"

"Discipline, then." And he grinned, suddenly and disarmingly. "I don't have much of that, either."

Meredith felt herself weakening beneath the spell of that lopsided, self-effacing and completely unpretentious grin. It was a gesture that begged to be returned, that touched a matching chord in her, that drew her close to him again and erased the boundaries of divergent opinions that had kept them so briefly apart. As much as she fought it, she felt a smile begin to tug at the corners of her own lips, and she shook her head helplessly. "Oh, Mark." She sighed. "How can you be so charming and so completely, totally, irretrievably wrong?"

"Are the two things mutually exclusive?" he inquired innocently. "Being charming and being right? I would have thought the opposite."

A small breath of laughter escaped her. "And in that case," she responded, "I guess you would have been right. All rogues are supposed to be charming, aren't they?"

"And black-hearted villains to the end," he agreed.

But the moment faded into seriousness again as Meredith looked at him, a small knot of hurt and confusion forming in her chest. She had so wanted him to be on her side. And he was—but because he liked her, not because he believed she was right. She wanted him to understand and support her, to understand how very, very important this was. "You really don't believe there's anything wrong with what they're doing, do you?" she inquired quietly. "You really can't see why I'm so upset."

"Darling . . ." The endearment slipped out easily, naturally, and it was accepted in the same way. "It's business. Remove all the mystical trappings and it comes down to one thing: money. Hell, yes, it's unethical, if you want to concern yourself with things like ethics, but you forget—I've lived in the world of high finance all my adult life, and there are few illusions left on Wall Street, believe me. Industry lets thousands of people go hungry for money. Bankers turn families out of homes for money. Governments start wars for money. It makes what these people are doing in the name of true enlightenment sound pretty small potatoes if you ask me.''

Meredith nodded slowly, bitterness tugging at her lips. She knew about the monetary aspects of the organization. "Kevin's trust fund," she said, and Mark nodded, understanding that, at least, without further explanation.

"Trust funds, college funds, donations from wealthy parents—the first rule of acceptance is to abandon all worldly goods."

The flash of angry incredulity in Meredith's eyes was unpreventable. "And you don't see anything wrong about that?"

"It's not blackmail, bribery or extortion," Mark pointed out calmly. "They're all over the age of consent before they're given permanent status. They make donations willingly. And besides, that's such a small part of the entire operation it's hardly even worth mentioning."

"Sure," responded Merry bitterly. "The rest of their assets come from selling flowers on the street and harassing little old ladies at the airport."

The cynical crease of Mark's lips was accompanied by a snort of laughter. "No, this organization is a lot classier than that. They're into big-time finance."

Merry's eyes narrowed sharply. "Like what?"

Mark glanced down at his glass again, shrugging. "Oh, I don't know. Real estate, stocks, bonds, growth industries..." And his eyes met hers plainly. "Look," he said, "all I'm saying is that as far as I can tell, the organization isn't into anything illegal and as a matter of fact has been a real boost to the economy around here. More people, more jobs, more jobs, more money, an endless circle. What is the harm in that?"

Oh, he was very persuasive. He made it sound so simple. So simple to be unconcerned, nonjudgmental, uncommitted, to see only black and white and care nothing for what lurked beneath the surface. But instead of irritating Merry, Mark's attitude only made her sad. Perhaps everything he said was true; perhaps she was being too emotional. But wasn't being too emotional better than having no emotions at all?

She looked at him, lounging on the floor with his long legs crossed at the ankles, weight resting on one elbow, eyes absently observing the patterns of sunlight in his wineglass. The faded denims fit him like a glove; the sloppy sweat shirt draped over his torso and left his neck bare. Meredith realized it was the first time she had ever seen Mark's throat. The throat, the most vulnerable part of the human animal, was always protected in defensive or uncertain situations, and Mark always kept his throat covered. Until now, in the security of his own home, with her.

when Mark handed her glass to her again. Merry lowered her legs to a crossed position on the cushion, tucking her skirt modestly between them. "There's one person we know for sure was being kept against her will. What do you have to say about that?"

A disturbed shadow came over Mark's eyes as he lowered himself to the cushion again, and he hesitated before replying. Meredith could almost see the various considerations that were flashing through his mind. That she had imagined the entire episode. That she was exaggerating. That her own state of emotional prejudice had allowed her to misunderstand. That it was an isolated incident that signified nothing. And then he shook his head slowly, sighing. "Ah, Merry," he said, a small, rueful smile touching his lips. "You make me think too much. The very thing I try so conscientiously to avoid."

"The very thing," Merry responded heavily, "that the Reverend Samuels refuses to allow at any cost."

Unexpectedly, Mark reached out and touched her cheek. Meredith's eyes flew to him in surprise, and Mark's smile was kind. "Look," he said, "you'll see Kevin Monday. You'll be better able to judge then whether or not your dire suspicions are correct. But until then, don't allow your—" he seemed to choose his words carefully "—resentment over the loss of your brother color your judgment. You're only making things more painful for yourself if you do."

How very reasonable he sounded. And how

very logical was his advice. Suppose Mark was right? Suppose Kevin's choice had been the best one for him? Who was she to sit in judgment upon the way another person chose to lead his life?

She remembered the way she had felt inside the temple that afternoon. Insulated, protected, content. Everyone there seemed happy. No conflicts, no hatred, no strife. Only peace and love. How could anyone condemn that?

But she shook her head determinedly, and she did not even realize she was speaking out loud. "There's something evil about that place," she said softly. "I feel it."

Mark let his hand drop and with a mild lift of the eyebrow pointed out, "Not a very persuasive argument from a person with your background."

Meredith shrugged uncomfortably, a small abashed grin stealing to the surface. "Now you know why I dropped out of law school. All emotion and no logic."

For a moment the gentle thoughtfulness in Mark's expression held her suspended. "There are worse things, I suppose," he said, and then the moment was gone. He grabbed her hand and pulled her to her feet. "However," he decided, "in this case I think your appalling lack of logic might be due to nothing more than two glasses of twenty-proof alcohol consumed on an empty stomach. Come along and watch the master gourmet at work."

Mark's kitchen was as open and airy as the rest of his apartment, though slightly better furnished.

The white walls were relieved by poppy-red appliances and a brick tile floor, butcher-block counter tops and a central work island. Once again, Meredith could not help wondering how many other women had perched upon the stool at that island and watched him prepare their dinner—and who they were.

"I still don't understand it," she confessed, leaning her chin on her palms as she watched him bring a head of lettuce and two oranges from the refrigerator to the island.

"Understand what?" He set the lettuce and the salad bowl before her and commanded, "Shred."

"Why you would want to live here. What about your social life?" she persisted shamelessly. It must have been the wine.

Mark smothered a grin as he began to peel the oranges over the garbage disposal. "I travel a lot in my job," he admitted. "If I get a craving for a fine restaurant or a good show, I can always find it. As for the other . . ." Now he looked at her with an ease and frankness that should have embarrassed Merry, but for some reason she felt too close to him to let it. "You might have guessed that relationships are not high on my list of priorities. One-night stands are more my style, and they're not hard to find."

She knew he was warning her, and she accepted it. But it hardly made any difference.

She shredded a fair amount of lettuce into the bowl and watched as Mark topped it with fresh orange slices, thin wisps of sweet onion, and a generous sprinkling of chopped almonds. "Strange salad," Merry commented as he placed the bowl in the refrigerator to chill.

He winked at her. "You are in for an entire orchestra of new experiences tonight, my dear," he replied, and the innocent comment sparked a little thrill along Merry's spine. It sounded like a promise of much more.

She sipped her wine and watched Mark work in the kitchen, fascinated with his simple movements and ordinary actions. The sleeves of his sweat shirt, pushed up above the elbows, revealed strong-boned wrists and lightly veined forearms. The hair on his arms was light brown. When he wiped his face with the back of his hand, he left a flour smudge on his cheek that Merry laughingly wiped off with a paper towel. For a moment as their eyes met, there was that spark of electricity again that made something flutter in Merry's stomach, and she quickly moved away.

The rich aromas of the meal he prepared seemed to be an extension of his personality—sensuous and elegant, refined yet flamboyant. And everything he did seemed to draw her closer to him.

A misty green-and-purple sunset lined the window by the time they carried salad bowls and plates to the octagonal table on the living-room floor, and Mark lit the red taper in the center. Its pinpoint brightness was a romantic contrast for the twilight-shadowed room and the muted colors that painted the window behind them. They sat again on the floor, Meredith tucking her skirt between her folded legs, and she inquired, "Do you always eat like this?"

"Minus the candle and with the accompaniment of the evening news, yes." And he grinned at her. "Sometimes I eat standing up," he admitted, "or sitting on my bed. The amount of dirty dishes and Chinese food containers in my bedroom would make you want to call the health department."

Merry laughed. "No, I mean—like this. Do you always cook for yourself?" She took a bite of her salad and widened her eyes in appreciation. The unlikely combination of flavors was set off by a delicate dressing, and the result was delicious.

"Hardly ever," he admitted. "But then..." And the spark in his eye took her back to her recent curiosity about his female companions. "I hardly ever have guests, either."

Merry refused to be embarrassed.

He served a magnificent concoction of eggs and fresh mushrooms smothered in a pungent cheese sauce on a bed of herb-buttered brown bread, and for a time Meredith was so involved with the enjoyment of her meal that she did not even try to make conversation.

"I take it you approve," Mark commented after a time and the spark in his eyes was teasing.

"Umm." Merry touched her napkin to her lips and took up her wineglass. "You can cook for me anytime."

"Next time," he responded, "you can cook for me."

Even as the little thrill of pleasure rose within her, it was tempered by a taste of disappointment. That was the kind of invitation that would be given by a man who was anticipating a long-term relationship. Other nights, other dinners, plenty of time... Even if Mark had been a different kind of man, even if the nonchalant words had been uttered with sincerity, there would be no other nights and no more opportunities. They were a self-limited happening and could look forward to nothing beyond the moment.

A vague, almost-sad little smile curved Meredith's lips as she took up her wineglass. "You know," she said, "it's funny. The way I ended up here... I certainly didn't expect to have any fun along the way. The circumstances are bizarre, the reasons for it tragic, but..." And a hint of shyness touched her smile as she glanced at him. "This is one of the most pleasant evenings I've spent in a long time." She lowered her eyes with a nervous little laugh and took a sip of her wine. "Who would have ever thought?" she added lightly, and looked back at him. His eyes were very deep, and soft. "I didn't even notice you when I first sat down next to you that night in the lounge," she admitted. "We never would have met if I hadn't been so bold as to order vodka in my Bloody Mary."

"Oh, I wouldn't bet on that," Mark said smoothly, and added a little more wine to her glass. "The reason you didn't notice me when you sat down was because I wasn't sitting there. I practically knocked a little old man in a business suit off the stool to sit beside you." And his eyes twinkled. "I wouldn't have let you leave that place without knowing I was there, believe me."

The laugh that bubbled to Merry's lips was both of startled nervousness and sheer pleasure. The movement he made to refill her glass had brought him very close, so that his arm brushed hers and his breath touched her cheek. She could see the spark of the candle flame in his eyes. "And what would you have done?" she teased, though a little breathlessly. "If you hadn't been inspired by the vodka, what would you have done to get my attention?"

"Oh, I don't know...." The rapid motion of his eyes across her face and downward brought a prickle of alertness to her skin. He lifted his fingers and lightly tucked a length of her hair behind her ear, letting his touch linger against the side of her neck. "Maybe this..." His head bent gracefully, and his lips brushed across her neck, near his fingers. "Or this..." She lost her breath with the tickling touch of his teeth against her earlobe. "Or maybe even this." His hand spread below her jawbone, steadying her face, and his lips hovered above hers. His tongue delicately traced the outline of her mouth.

The fever spread over Merry's skin, brightening her eyes, sharpening her pulse, suspending her breath. She whispered, trying to tease, "That would have certainly gotten my attention!" But she was not sure she actually made any sound at all, because in the next moment the full pressure of his lips descended upon hers.

The glass of wine was no longer in her hand, and the fingers that had held it were circling around his back, tracing the outline of warmth and muscles the soft material of the sweat shirt protected, drawing him closer. The heat of the candle flame seemed to have infused itself into her body, or perhaps it was generated from him, because he seemed to be wrapped around her, enfolding all her senses with his presence, blending into her and absorbing her. She was aware of every separate sensation: the softness of his lips; the slow, exquisitely exploratory nature of his kiss; the strength of his fingers sheltering her face; the gradual tightening of his muscles as his other arm slipped around her waist, cradling her. The shape of his thigh, pressed against hers. The warmth of his chest upon her breasts as he brought her gradually against him. The texture of his hair, like individual strands of woven silk beneath her fingers. The blending of wine-scented breaths, the skip and race of escalating pulses, the tingling pulse of every separate nerve cell, the winding sensation of breathless wonder and urgent anticipation that coiled below her breastbone. Yet as a whole she knew only him, the beauty of a kiss that was just as she had imagined it would be from the moment she first saw him, the blending of bodies and needs and personalities that strained for each other, that fit together. And it was wonderful. More than she had expected, more than she deserved, far more than was wise.

His lips left hers slowly, but there was no sense of deprivation, only a dazed wonder that promised more. She felt his smile curve against her cheek. "I think," he murmured, "that we were meant for each other. And I think I knew it the first moment I saw you.'' He lifted his face a little to look down at her, his fingers caressing her neck. His eyes, reflecting the candlelight, were lazy, as dark as velvet and just as soft. ''That frightens me a little,'' he said huskily.

''Me, too,'' she whispered, but the arch of her throat was too much of a temptation for him; his lips came down to explore it delicately.

She felt reason and logic slowly slip away on the dizzy threads of pleasure generated by the butterfly touches of his lips and tongue. She had known it would happen. She had known all along that once in the arms of this man, resistance and will would melt away beneath the demands of self-indulgent pleasure. And she knew why. It was the vacation syndrome. Away from home, in a strange environment and under the influence of unfamiliar stimuli, it was only natural to let one's guard down a little, to seek new adventures, to behave in a way one normally would not under normal circumstances. To think in terms not of consequences but of gratification, to see only the immediate, not the long-range. Meredith knew she could not afford to get involved with Mark Brasfield. She knew it would not end with one night of pleasure. Already she was far too involved with him to let him go with a casual goodbye when the time came; she could not afford to complicate her life more. Not now, not when so much was at stake....

She felt the brush of his hand upon her ankle, smooth warm fingers tracing the shape of her calf and her knee and her thigh where it curved close to her body beneath her skirt, and she went weak. She knew the quickening of his breath against the bare flesh of her chest, which was exposed by the slightly scooped bodice, and the fresh scent of his hair in her nostrils. Her fingertips threaded through his hair, felt the heat of skin at the back of his neck and explored the circle of a gold chain until it disappeared beneath his sweat shirt. She wanted to follow the course of that chain, to feel the muscles of his bare chest against her palms, to bury her face in the rich warm scent of his hair and to discover with her lips the sensitive hollow of his throat, the lobe of his ear and that little crease at the corner of his mouth. She wanted to learn of him, all of him, and to give pleasure to him, and it was with more strength of will than she thought she possessed that she caught his hand and moved away.

He met her eyes with the hazy cloud of question and the lingering light of passion in his own, and it was a moment before Merry could speak. She had to swallow hard, several times, to clear her voice, and even then she could not look at him. "I think," she managed after a moment, nervously spreading the folds of her skirt to cover more of her legs, "that it might be better if you took me back to my hotel now."

When she tried to withdraw her hand, he held it firm, and he inquired gently, "Do you really want to do that?"

Merry looked at him, her gaze steady, her eyes an open window to all she was feeling, all she was thinking. "No," she answered, not quite evenly.

"I don't really want to. But I think I should."

A slow smile, a mixture of puzzlement and regret, softened his face. He looked at her as though he could not quite believe what he was seeing but as though every part of it filled him with wonder. "Oh, Merry," he murmured helplessly, and he dropped his eyes. "You are so incredibly honest! How in the world did you ever get mixed up with me?"

He brought their entwined hands to his lips; he touched her knuckles with a kiss. His smile was kind and reassuring. "So tell me, love," he invited softly. "Why do you think you should do this thing you really don't want to do?"

Merry's answering smile was a little weak, and it vanished quickly. This time, when she attempted to withdraw her hand, Mark offered no resistance. "It's complicated," she began, and then did not know how to continue. She linked her fingers together in her lap and dropped her eyes to study them.

"These things usually are," Mark supplied helpfully.

"It's just that," she continued in a rush, deciding just to blurt it out and be done with it, "I met you two days ago. I don't know you at all. I'm just passing through here, and I'll never see you again. I have too much on my mind right now to get tangled up in a love affair. And I'm not really experienced enough to tell the difference between love and lust, and one-night stands are not for me. That's all."

Mark released his breath slowly, regarding her

with cautious admiration. "Well," he said, "that just about covers it, doesn't it?" His lips tilted up wryly at one corner. "Whoever told you you couldn't argue a case was out of his mind. And here am I, practiced perpetuator of one-night stands, without a thing to say."

And then his hand lifted slowly to her face; he grasped a strand of hair that glistened like gold against her cheek and smoothed it back with a caressing stroke of his fingers. "Except, perhaps," he added gently, "that just because it's temporary doesn't necessarily mean it's bad. Maybe you could think about that."

His closing argument was very persuasive. Think about it? She would think about nothing else. She turned away quickly before he could read it in her eyes and reached for her shoes. "The dinner was delicious, Mark. . . ."

"And so was the conversation, and so was the company," he added, making her smile. "Stay for dessert?" he coaxed. "Chocolate chip ice cream," he reminded her.

She leaned forward to slip on her shoes, and her hair fell over her shoulder, hiding the dimpling smile. "I'm tempted, but—"

He caught her hair and moved it away from her face, bending to catch her expression. "Maybe another time?"

Her smile gentled, and her eyes told him entirely too much. "Maybe," she said softly, and he seemed to accept that.

Mark parked by the side entrance of the hotel, near the park. He held her hand as they walked up the flower-lined path that separated the hotel property from the park, and it was very quiet. Early on Saturday evening the only signs of life came from within the hotel itself, as though everyone had drawn their shutters upon the temptations of the life that waited outside...just as Merry should do, she reminded herself firmly. She should protect herself from the temptation of this man. She should be strong enough to shield her emotions, as Mark did, to close off access to her heart, as he was so easily able to do.

But the moonlight was soft, Mark's arm around her shoulders warm. The brave little tulips lining the walk looked like statuary reproductions, and the scent of the night was sweet. And in the lingering shadows before they reached the lighted entranceway, Mark bent and kissed her. It was a sweet kiss, a gentle kiss that said no more than good night, and when it was over, his finger lingered against her face, stroking her cheek.

"Sure you won't change your mind about that ice cream?" he invited softly.

"I'm sure," she whispered back. But she wasn't sure. Not about anything.

Mark's tender smile understood but did not press. He brought her fingers again briefly to his lips, a gallant Old World gesture that melted her heart. "Good night, Merry," he said.

Merry stood there for a long time after he had gone, watching the place where he had been, feeling the scent and the touch on her body. Wishing...

And then she caught a glimpse of something

out of the corner of her eye. It was a man lurking in the shadows of the corner of the building a few yards away. His stance was furtive, his dark plaid shirt and jeans blending into the night and making him almost invisible, except for the glow of a cigarette. Meredith was uncannily certain the man had been watching them.

And then, before she could call out a challenge or move a step toward him, he tossed away the cigarette and moved quickly away from her, disappearing around the corner of the building toward the front parking lot. But not before she caught a glimpse of his face.

It was the man Mark had introduced to her that afternoon as Brother Chi.

Chapter Seven

Stonington closed down tight on Sunday morning, just as any good little town in the heart of the Bible Belt should. Stores were shuttered, streets were empty, businesses locked. But Meredith found the stillness eerie. There was a subdued atmosphere in the hotel dining room when she went down for breakfast, and it was mostly empty. Perhaps it was the tolling of the church bells she missed the most. She remembered with a jolt that it was another thing the town seemed to be missing on her brief tour of it the previous day... churches.

Was it possible that the Source of Enlightenment was powerful enough to drive all other churches away from its borders? If so, where did all the people who lived in the town go to worship? Or perhaps they didn't. Perhaps they just sat at home smiling their blank little smiles until someone came along on Monday morning to wind them up again.

Meredith knew she had to get out of there. The stillness was driving her crazy. She remembered passing a twenty-four-hour convenience store on her way into town—about ten miles down the highway, actually—and she thought she might be able to replace her lipstick there or perhaps pick up a few magazines or even a contraband novel or two. At least it would give her something to do.

She wondered if she would see Mark that day.

It occurred to Merry that if everything went well the next day with Kevin, she could leave that place before the sun went down and never see Mark again. Why did that possibility disturb her so? How could she possibly have come to care for him so much in such a short time?

Because he was here, that's all, the little-used logical part of her mind told her. *Because he was with you in a time of unusual circumstances and high stress and naturally his importance became exaggerated to you. He's the only friend you have in town. Naturally you depend on him. He's the most attractive man you've ever met in your life. Of course you want him. But it's all just a trick of circumstances. You won't even miss him that much when you're gone. You won't really think about him all the time. You're not falling in love with him....*

But the real Merry, the intuitive and emotional and completely illogical Merry, was very much afraid that she was.

It was good to get out of the town. The moment she passed the city limits, the atmosphere seemed to lighten, to become bright. Merry actually breathed easier, and she had a very dim impulse to just keep on driving, heading west, past the Kansas border and onward, putting miles between her and Stonington and never looking back again. Merry had seen a movie one time in which the perfect little middle America town was filled with perfect little saltbox houses and perfect husbands in business suits and housewives in aprons and children who never got dirty and in which everyone was smiling all the time. And it turned out that there was nothing beneath the plastic skin of those people except wires and silicone chips. She had seen another movie in which an entire town was populated by zombies. Merry gave an elaborate shudder and concentrated on her driving, trying not to think about movies.

The store she sought was closer to fifteen miles away than ten, but the drive was good for her. She felt a lot more clearheaded and competent than she had at any time since arriving in Stonington. She was letting her imagination get the better of her, she knew. Mark was right; there was nothing evil about the town or the church. Bizarre, perhaps. Unethical, most definitely. But it was nothing she could not handle. She would not let it intimidate her anymore.

Merry enjoyed browsing around, taking her time and enjoying the atmosphere of real civilization for a change. She could not find the exact color of lipstick she wanted, but she was adventurous enough to try a change, and she selected a bottle of nail polish to match. She picked up a couple of magazines and promised satisfaction to her sweet tooth with a handful of chocolate bars.

She was paying for her purchases when she caught a glimpse of what appeared to be a familiar figure. She turned around, and there was no mistake about it. It was definitely the woman from the motel, the one Mark referred to as "old Maud."

Meredith did not know what persuaded her to do it. Perhaps it was her renowned stubborn streak. Perhaps it was no more than the lingering sense of insult that would not let an injustice go unrequited. She waited at the door until Maud made to pass, and then she stepped deliberately in front of her.

"Good morning," Merry said pleasantly. "Do you remember me?"

Meredith saw instantly in the other woman's eyes that she did. First there was startled recognition, then contempt, then simple anger as Maud squared her shoulders and attempted to push past.

Of course, ignoring her was worse than insulting her, and Meredith had no intention of letting the woman just walk away without an explanation. She reached out to catch her sleeve. "Now wait just a minute," she demanded. The humiliation of the scene at the motel was sweeping over her again, refueling her indignation. "I want to know what you have against me. I've never done anything to you. You have no right—"

The woman fastened a burning look upon the place where Merry's hand touched her arm and then turned that gaze, lively with hatred, upon Merry herself. It was almost enough to make Merry back away. "You and your kind," she spat out, "killed my husband! Isn't that enough to hold against you?"

"What?" The word was barely a whisper from shocked lips. Merry let her hand fall away, staring at the woman. Maud turned and strode away with a look that would imprint itself forever on Merry's mind, and it took a moment for Meredith to even gather her senses enough to follow her. When she did, it was with a surge of adrenaline and determination, and she repeated louder, more incredulously, "*What*?" She pushed upon the glass door after Maud and followed her onto the sidewalk. "I don't even know your husband!" she declared, moving in front of her again. "What are you talking about?"

Maud fixed her with one last coldly penetrating look. "You're with that damn church, aren't you?" she demanded. "Church!" she repeated with a snort. "If you can call it that. Ruining innocent people's lives, breaking up homes, driving hardworking folks out of what's rightfully theirs." Her eyes narrowed sharply on Merry. "That's what killed my John, and nothing else! Fighting you, worrying about you, working himself right into a heart attack—"

"No!" Merry shook her head furiously, as much to free herself from the dazed shock this new influx of information had caused as in denial. "I'm not with the church," she insisted. "My brother—he's one of the converts, and I've come to see him, that's all, to try to get him to come back with me if I can. What are you talking about? Whose lives were ruined? Why do you think they're responsible for your husband's death? Please tell me!"

The woman looked at her long and hard, as though trying to decide for herself whether or not Merry was telling the truth. And in the end Merry still did not know whether Maud believed her. "If your brother's there," she said, "you might as well give up on him." And she turned to go.

"No." Again Merry caught her arm, and Maud turned. There was not quite the same amount of contempt in her eyes this time, only cautious curiosity. "Please," Merry said softly. "Please tell me what you know. It might help me to save my brother."

For a long moment Maud appeared to be undecided. Perhaps it was something in Merry's expression that convinced her, or it might have been nothing more than the need to talk to someone about it. She said, "Three years ago they started coming in, buying up property, putting up their buildings, taking over the banks. Before we knew it, they owned half the county, then started taking over the town. Jonathan, he owned the newspaper, and he put up a good fight. He was one of the last to hold out." A gleam of proud memory came into her eyes and was quickly extinguished by bitterness. "But when they own your mortgage and your advertisers and your subscribers, there's not too much you can do. In the end they burned him out." Merry's eyes widened, and Maud nodded grimly. "Oh, yes, that's what it was all right. They called in an accident, but what they were after were his records...just like with the library and the town hall. They didn't want anything left to remind people what it was like before they came along."

Merry stared at her, a sick feeling washing over her with the Orwellian implications of it all. Erase history and you can recreate it. Erase the past and you can make people believe anything you want them to.

"I . . . don't understand," she managed in a moment, a little weakly. "Do you mean to say that the church owns the whole town?"

Maud nodded. "The whole county," she specified. "Every square inch of it. When their homes and businesses were gone, most everybody moved out; the few that stayed changed. Started going out to that temple, taking jobs in town, halfway believing, I guess, all that falderal they're teaching out there. And a lot of new people moved in. A few of us, we stayed close by, and we remember how it used to be. It's like a damn ghost town, I tell you. It gives me the willies to even go in there anymore."

Incredible, Meredith thought dazedly. An organization moves in, buys out businesses, infiltrates itself into the culture, changes and recreates a whole town . . . Then she remembered that hated elliptical symbol that had become to her a sign of contamination and evil—it was on the hotel stationery, on the menus. She had seen it engraved into at least one cornerstone and emblazoned in very tiny print on shop windows. It gave her a cold chill, thinking about it. She should have put it all together before.

"And that's not the worst of it," Maud told her confidently. "What's happened here in Stonington is just a part of it. They've got bases all over the country, you know. You should have heard Jonathan talk about it. He was on to some things."

"What things?" Merry insisted with sudden urgency. She did not know why she was pushing. She knew more than she wanted to already. What could she do about any of this, anyway? All she wanted was her brother.... "Can you remember?"

The unfamiliar smile that curved Maud's heavily painted lips was regretful. "Not that would make any sense, I'm afraid. He left some papers, a few files that he kept at home that the fire missed. I thought about trying to put them together and publishing them after he died, but I couldn't make anything out of them."

"I have some legal experience," Merry said, hoping that would impress her. "Perhaps if I looked..."

For a moment Maud hesitated. And then she said with a shrug, "Can't see that it would do any harm. But," she added quietly and firmly, "nothing's going to help your brother if they've got him."

Merry refused to believe that. She simply refused to.

LATE IN THE AFTERNOON Merry was still poring over the files that were spread over her bed. As

Maud had predicted, nothing about them made much sense at first glance. There were newspaper clippings relating to the establishment of branches of the operation in various cities. There was a manuscript-form copy of an article that had apparently never been published in the Stonington *Gazette* that expounded the theory that the Source of Enlightenment was at the time one of the most powerful financial networks in the country. There were copies of legal documents referring to various corporations. And in one fat file upon which Jonathan had scrawled in thick, heavy-handed letters the one word "Astra" were handwritten notes that Merry finally began to understand related to some corporate financial activity. Maud told her that it was the file he had been working on at the time of his heart attack two months earlier and that he seemed very excited about what he was discovering. But whatever it was, he had died before he could put it on paper.

The first page in the Astra file was a list of Middle Eastern countries with which, presumably, the Source of Enlightenment had financial dealings. That made her more than a little uneasy. It meant that the influence of the church extended beyond national boundaries, for one thing. And it meant a financial power had established a base in the economy of some very politically unstable countries, which, to Merry's way of thinking, spelled *danger* in flashing letters. But there was no law against that, was there? Many reputable American corporations had branches in the

Middle East, to everyone's profit. That couldn't have been what Jonathan was so excited about... could it?

By four o'clock her mind was whirling with facts and figures. The overall picture was not hard to put together: the Source of Enlightenment was, as Mark had pointed out, merely a tax-exempt shelter for a business. It was composed of multitudinous corporations, many of them dummy, Merry was sure, whose interests ranged from real estate to agriculture. The number of banks it controlled alarmed her. But none of that would have been surprising to Jonathan, who had watched these people swallow up a whole town in a matter of a few years. He had been on to something bigger; Merry was sure of it.

And Merry had a nagging feeling that whatever it was, it had something to do with the church's holdings in the Middle East. It was something so obvious a blind man could have seen it, but to her increasing frustration, the connection continued to elude Merry. She just didn't have enough information, or she simply wasn't imaginative enough to put it all together.

The jarring of the telephone shocked her out of her deep ruminations, and the sound of Roger's voice on the other end of the line was so disorienting that at first she did not even make the connection. Then his laughing enjoinder, "You do remember me, don't you?" startled her back to present consciousness.

"Roger!" she exclaimed. "Good heavens, it's just that I wasn't expecting to hear from you!"

"Your mother gave me the number. I kept expecting you to call, but . . ." The explicit reproach in his voice needed no further explanation.

"I'm sorry." She placed the sheaf of papers she had carried with her to the telephone on the desk and pulled out the chair. "It's just that there's been so much—"

"That's exactly what I want to hear about. What's been going on?"

Merry had not before even considered what a relief it would be to put it all into words for someone in the real world. Once she started, she couldn't seem to stop herself, beginning with her hostile greeting at the service station, through the vandalism of her room, then up to her conversation with Maud that afternoon.

"Roger, you never told me," she interrupted herself for an editorial. "You never told me this place was so weird! Do you realize they've taken over the whole town—not just physically but mentally, as well. Everyone who lives here is a carbon copy of the people out at that temple." Almost everyone, she amended herself silently, thinking of Mark. "And they have no opposition, none whatsoever! Can you imagine," she said, her voice falling a little with dread awe, "what kind of power it takes to do something like that?"

Roger's voice was sharp with concentration. "And this woman—Maud?—you said she gave you some information about the organization's larger scale?"

Merry nodded enthusiastically, taking up the

papers on the desk. "Of course their holdings are enormous. I already told you that. A lot of dummy corporations. But what Jonathan—that's Maud's husband—seemed to be most interested in was something to do with the stock market. Roger, does the word 'Astra' mean anything to you?"

Roger was silent for a long time. She remembered his perpetual habit of taking notes over the telephone, and Merry wasn't surprised. At last he said, "Why? What is it?"

"It's just the label on this folder about the stock market. Is there anything on the exchange listed under that name?"

"I don't know. It would be easy enough to check out, I guess." But Roger sounded terse, distracted, and she should have known what was coming. "Listen, Merry, I think you should get out of there." His tone held the unmistakable finality of an order. "Apparently you've stumbled into something way over your head and you—"

"What?" she demanded, stubbornness coming out as belligerence in her voice. "Nothing that wasn't here long before I came and—"

"You've been threatened twice. Your room has been broken into—"

"That's nothing!" *Damn,* she thought. She should have known Roger would react that way. So overprotective, such a mother hen. He had been against her coming in the first place. He had warned her she couldn't just expect to waltz in here and have easy access to Kevin and all that sealed him from the outside world. Well, she did have access now—to her brother and a lot more—and she wasn't about to back off.

"I am not leaving here until I see Kevin," she told him firmly. "And meanwhile I'm going to try to find out everything I can about this Astra business. Roger, these people have got to be stopped! This might be a way to do it."

"There you go again, jumping off the deep end. Do you really think if there was anything questionable going on with an organization this big, it could have stayed in power for twenty-five years? Don't you think someone would have discovered it long before now? A fine time you picked to have ambition!"

That stung. "I'm going to stay here," Meredith said stiffly, "and do what I came to do. Are you going to help or not?"

There was a long silence. "All right," Roger said at last. "What do you want me to do?"

"Just find out everything you can about the organization. See if you can find out what this Astra business is. And call me back."

"I'll do what I can," Roger said heavily. "And Merry—will you for heaven's sake be careful?"

Merry hung up the phone more disturbed than she wanted to admit. Could Roger be right? Was she once again coloring the facts with her own point of view? What did any of it have to do with the real reason she was there—to see Kevin. So the organization was powerful. There were a lot of powerful organizations in the world. Just because this one had a bizarre foundation did not necessarily mean there was anything basically wrong with the way they conducted their business. And if there was, what did she think she could do about it. What difference did it make to her or to Kevin?

But eventually her wandering thoughts were drawn back to the files on her bed. She went over and sat in the midst of them again, frowning. Dummy corporations. Stock Market. What connection had the newspaperman seen between the two that was so important he had worked himself into a heart attack over it?

An hour later her eyes ached, and her brain felt like one huge overused muscle. She couldn't make any sense of it. She went over to the window and looked out at the park; it was very still, almost deserted. The few people who sat under the fall of spring sunshine were like motionless mannequins; reading, mostly, or simply sitting alone in quiet contemplation of the day. The entire picture had a photographic quality to it, like something reproduced and not real.

A knock on her door startled Merry. Roger's disapproving warnings had done nothing to ease her paranoia, and she approached the door cautiously, putting the chain on before she opened it a crack. A panoply of color and scent blossomed into the opening.

With a soft exclamation of delight, Merry closed the door, removed the chain and then flung it open again. Mark thrust a bouquet of multicolored spring blossoms into her arms. "A replacement for the vodka," he explained. "I thought these, at least, they'd let you keep in your room."

Merry laughed out loud, and in an impulsive gesture of happiness and relief, flung her arms around him and hugged him briefly. "Just what I needed!" she exclaimed. "Thank you!"

The startled softening of Mark's eyes expressed surprise over the depth of her appreciation, but just as he brought his hands up to her waist, Meredith recovered herself and stepped away. A self-conscious flush stained her cheeks, but the brightness of her eyes did not fade. It was so good to see him. He was just what she needed—the sight of him, so clean and beautiful, the touch of him, so strong and sure. Just Mark's being there was all she needed to take her mind off her brooding thoughts and assure that there was, indeed, something right with the world.

His finger came up to trace the shape of her cheek in that tender gesture that was so characteristic of him, one she had learned to expect and anticipate, and the hazy light in his eyes made her heart skip a beat. "I should have brought the whole greenhouse," he said softly, and those eyes moved downward with widening delight to her lips, where they rested like a kiss.

Merry tossed him a quick, vibrant smile and stepped away. "I'll find something to put these in," she said a little breathlessly.

What she found was the coffeepot that had been sent up with room service for lunch, and she rinsed and filled it with water in the bathroom. The day suddenly had taken on a whole new perspective. Mark was there. He hadn't forgotten her. She had not realized how that concern had nagged at the back of her mind all day, that after the previous night he might have begun to see the futility of continuing their association, that he might have decided there was no sense following a dead-end course, that she had made herself entirely too clear about what he could expect from their relationship. That it might have been better all around had he simply given up did not rise to trouble her now that he was there. It only mattered that he hadn't given up, and she was glad.

When she came back, dripping water from the improvised vase and arranging little sprigs of baby's breath more artfully among the daisies and carnations, he was standing by her bed, curiously glancing at the scattered papers there. "What's all this?" he inquired.

Merry set the vase on the dresser with a thump, spilling more water, and whirled. "You *are* just the person I needed to see!" she exclaimed excitedly. Why hadn't she thought about it before? Mark was the financier; Mark was the stock-market expert; Mark was the connection who could put this all together for her and give her access to any further information she needed. Why hadn't she thought about it before?

She went over to the bed, crawling to the middle of it to search for the papers she needed, sitting on her knees as she told him, "You remember Maud? The woman who owns the motel outside of town?" He nodded, the curiosity in his expression mixed with amusement over her inexplicable enthusiasm. "Did you know her husband owned the newspaper that used to be here?"

Mark shrugged, removing a pile of papers from the edge of the bed where he intended to sit and glancing at them absently before handing them to Merry. "I guess so. What has that got to do with—"

"These are some of his records," Merry explained. And then, her brow creasing with disturbance, she added, "Mark, you never told me how the church took over this town, closing up businesses, burning people out—"

An incredulous amusement shone in Mark's eyes as he sat on the edge of the bed. "Is that what she told you?"

"The newspaper office did burn down," Merry defended. "And the organization did close him down."

"Think a minute, darling," he persuaded, his eyes twinkling tolerantly. "Why would they want to burn down something they already owned?"

"For the records," Meredith replied firmly, thrusting the file toward him. "Investigative records that Maud's husband was compiling on the organization's business affairs. Financial affairs, to be more precise," she specified grandly, "and that's where you come in."

The startled look Mark shot her completely erased any lingering mirth from his eyes. He accepted the folder hesitantly. "What do you mean?"

"Just look," she commanded.

Mark gave her one more wary glance and then opened the folder.

As hard as she tried, Merry could read nothing

from his expression as he turned pages, scanning their contents without comment. His face was perfectly blank, registering neither comprehension, recognition, disapproval nor shock—just nothing. Merry might as well have shown him a text written in another language.

At last, his silence became unnerving, and Merry insisted impatiently, "Don't you see? He was trying to make some connection between these dummy corporations and stock-market investments—"

"Not stocks," murmured Mark absently, "commodities."

So he was paying attention, after all. Merry's triumph was short-lived, however, as Mark closed the folder and handed it back to her, perfectly blank-eyed. "So?" he said. "What do you want from me?"

For a moment Merry was taken aback. What, indeed? What had she expected Mark to be able to make of the information that she had not already deciphered for herself? "Well," she began, stammering a little, "could you—well, couldn't you maybe tell me what kinds of stocks—commodities—" she corrected herself, "they're heavily invested in? And maybe why? And this Astra thing—do you know what it is? Is it on the exchange?"

With a motion so abrupt it startled her, Mark stood up and strode a few feet away from her. When he turned back to her, his expression was filled with incredulity and impatience. "For heaven's sake, Merry," he exclaimed, "what difference does it make? What are you trying to prove, anyway? You've got a bunch of information—" he gestured derisively toward the folders on her bed "—that you have no business having, that means nothing and that doesn't even pertain to you! It's none of your business! What is it with you, anyway?"

Merry got to her feet, hurt by his unexpected onslaught but stung into defensive anger. "It *is* my business," she shot back. "If they're up to something illegal—"

"Damn it, you have no proof of anything illegal!" he returned. His eyes were sparking with repressed anger and disgust. "You have no proof of anything. You're after these people because of some noble vendetta of your own that has nothing to do with what's legal or illegal. You go flying off on some farfetched crusade that has nothing whatsoever to do with you! Why do you want to get involved?"

Merry had never seen Mark angry before, and for a man of such low-key emotions it was an awesome sight to behold. That his anger was directed at her made it even harder to deal with, and she felt the inexplicable sting of tears in her eyes as she shouted back, "Because I care, that's why! Because for once in my life I care enough about something, and believe enough in something, to get involved even if it is inconvenient, even if it does cause trouble for me. But of course I couldn't expect a man like you to understand anything about being *involved*!"

The last word, to her horror, was choked on

something that sounded very much like a sob, and recognition of the fact registered with a softening in Mark's face. Merry turned away angrily, scrubbing at the dampness around her eyes, when Mark took a step toward her.

"Ah, Merry..." His voice, gentle with regret, fell upon her like a caress, and he took her shoulders lightly. "Honey, I'm sorry. I didn't mean to yell at you. It's just that you're so damn exasperating with your one-track mind." She could feel the coaxing, apologetic smile in his voice, but it did not urge a return from her. "Listen. Merry, look at me."

Though still soft, his tone was serious, and he crooked his forefinger beneath her chin, turning her face to his. She met his gaze defiantly, refusing to lift her hand to brush away the remnants of angry tears that still lingered on her lashes. It disturbed her greatly when Mark lifted his finger and performed the task for her. There was such tenderness in the motion that she almost started crying again.

"Merry," he said soberly, "don't get angry again, but don't you think the real reason you've become so militant about this thing is because it's the first noble and completely unselfish thing you've ever done?" And at the protest he saw forming, he lifted a warning finger close to her lips. "Because this is your chance to prove to your parents, and to yourself, that you can do the responsible thing, the right thing, and make everyone proud of you? And don't you think that with all that behind you, you've maybe exaggerated the importance of your cause a little bit? Come on," he persuaded gently, "let's see some of that renowned honesty that impresses me so much about you."

Merry wanted to argue with him, to defend herself and her principles, but in the end she had to drop her eyes. How could one defend the passions of a cause to someone who saw only in black and white and who didn't even care when the line blurred toward gray? And of course he was right. Her motivations were not entirely pure. She had chosen to do this for her parents' sake as much as for Kevin's, to gain their approval, to show them that she could act in behalf of someone other than herself on occasion and that she could do the right thing when action was called for. But that was only part of it. There was substance behind her mission. She cared about the outcome, and there was a wrong to be righted here.

Merry turned away from him with a sigh. "Oh, Mark," she said tiredly, helplessly, "don't you believe in anything?"

"No" was his simple, unhesitant reply.

The strained half smile she gave him was more of an attempt to cheer herself up than anything else. "Not even yourself?"

"Especially not myself," he assured her, and his smile was wry and unpretentious. "I know myself too well."

Merry's expression grew curious as she tilted her head toward him, studying him. "You keep the information well hidden," she observed thoughtfully. "Sometimes I wish I could see what really lies behind that mask of indifference you're so good at.''

For a moment there was a flicker of something like surprise in his eyes, but it was gone quickly. He merely answered, "Why?"

Mark was manipulating her out of the intensity of the previous scene, playing with casual banter until she relaxed, and Meredith knew it. And it was working.

"Why not?" she challenged back.

"Too much knowledge can be a dangerous thing" was his typically enigmatic reply.

But Merry was relentless in her probing. She wandered over to the dresser and perched upon its edge, her hands folded studiously in her lap. "Try me," she invited mildly. "What would I find out if I knew you as well as you know yourself?"

Mark came over to her, relaxing in the game. "That I am a man totally without scruples," he responded. "That I don't know the difference between right and wrong and wouldn't care if I did. That the only things I value are those that can be turned into cold hard cash. That I am completely self-serving and self-absorbed. That—" He was close to her now, and his eyes were dark and clear, his words very deliberate. He took her hands and held them lightly in both of his. "I am not a nice man, and you would be a fool to trust me."

But as she looked into his eyes, felt the gentle security of his hands holding hers, it hardly seemed to matter. The small, rueful smile came unbidden to her lips, and almost without realizing what she was doing, she exerted an increasing pressure upon his hands that brought him closer, his thighs meeting the edge of the dresser and flanked on either side by her own, his chest separated from hers only by the distance of their entwined hands. "I guess I'm a fool then." She sighed and bent her head forward until her forehead rested against his shoulder.

Mark's hands released hers and came around her, gently caressing the fall of her hair and the shape of her back beneath the thin material of the T-shirt. She felt his lips upon her hair and the flutter of his breath that played against her scalp. "Ah, Merry," he murmured. "So intense, so stubborn, so self-justified ... What am I going to do with you?"

Just love me, she thought, and her arms moved around his waist, bringing him closer. She turned her cheek to his chest, and her eyes closed tightly with the depth of her need. *Just hold me and love me and don't ever let me go.*

The muscles of his chest were warm and pliant beneath the cotton material of his shirt. Her hand moved over his back languorously, loving the shape of it beneath her fingers, loving the feel of him against her. He moved her hair away from her neck, and his lips clasped the bare flesh there tenderly, lingeringly. Then his hand moved down to discover the fullness of her breast, circling and cupping it, lifting it to meet the warm pressure of lips that followed.

The wonder of engorging need enfolded Merry with the warm pressure that penetrated her T-shirt. The gentle erotic motions of his tongue

and teeth discovered her shape and caressed it as
the firm pressure of his hand molded and cupped.
There was weakness, and there was electricity;
there was the paralyzing suffusion of need. There
was the heavy sensation of mindless pleasure and
the building ache for more of him that she knew
this time she would be unable to resist.

Her soft moan was a sound of invitation, and
her hands came up to caress his hair; her face
moved close to his, tasting the warmth of his
temple and the edge of his ear with flickering motions of her tongue. She felt his indrawn breath
against the damp material that covered her breast
and sensed the tautening of his muscles as he
lifted his head and brought his hands down the
length of her back, beneath her buttocks, lifting
her off the dresser and bringing her against him.

His eyes were bright and opaque, infinitely alert,
quietly promising. His fingers were firm against
her buttocks, pressing her into the strength of his
pelvis; she could feel the irregular beat of his heart
against hers. But there was no other sign of need
or urgency on a face that was schooled to conceal
emotions as he inquired huskily, "Merry, love,
are you sure you know what you're doing?"

She could feel herself being drawn into his eyes.
Those eyes, so deep, so observant, giving him
easy access to the depths of her soul while protecting his own from being touched by her.

Yes, she knew. She knew she was giving in to
what she wanted instead of what she knew was
best. She knew that this man was wrong for her.
They were poles apart in their values and their

thinking, and nothing could come of it but heart-break. There was no chance for them. This thing had no permanence. It would hurt when they parted. She knew she was succumbing to emotion and not reason; she knew this could possibly be the cruelest thing she had ever done to herself. She knew she was being impulsive and self-indulgent. And she knew she loved him.

Merry brought her hands up to rest on either side of his neck, cupping his face. Her eyes were very steady. "Mark," she said softly, "I wish you believed in what I'm trying to do. I wish you understood, and I wish you cared...about a lot of things. But as long as you're on my side, as long as you're my friend, it's enough. Nothing else matters."

And then those eyes were suddenly shielded from her; he brought his forehead slowly to rest against hers. She could feel something change within him, the forceful relaxation of his muscles, the loosening of the hold of his fingers, the almost deliberate slowing of his heartbeat. And he drew a heavy breath. "Oh, no, you don't, lady," he said softly, and he stepped away.

It took a moment for Merry's confused senses to register the absence of him, and even then it took a time longer for her to believe it. One moment he had been holding her, every part of him infusing itself into her; one moment they had been ready to make love to each other, and the next her arms were empty, and he was walking away from her.

She made an automatic half gesture to reach for

him. "What?" Her voice sounded breathless and not quite steady. "What did I do?"

Mark ran his fingers through his hair with an uncharacteristically tense motion, and when he looked back at her, the dry quirk of his smile was forced. "Got too close, that's all."

He released another unsteady breath and crossed to the window in three even strides, as though anxious to put distance between them. Then he turned abruptly, bracing his hands against the windowsill, elbows stiff, shoulders straight. His face was taut despite the easiness of his tone. "Look," he said plainly. "All I ever wanted was to take you to bed. I don't think I exactly tried to keep it a secret from you, either. You walked into that lounge, and every animal part of me came alive— There you were, tall, blond and gorgeous, quite different from the usual fare served around here, right? You were probably the most striking woman I've ever seen, and I knew right then I had to have you. As an extra added bonus, you even had a personality, and I started to like you." He shrugged. "Great, I thought. Somebody I can get along with outside of bed as well as in. And the best part was, you were just passing through, a stranger I never had to see again, a built-in one-night stand. What could be more perfect?"

Merry could not tell by his tone or his expression whether or not he was trying to shock her. His stance against the window looked defensive. The slight prominence of a muscle in his jaw could have been belligerent, but Merry was not shocked or disappointed. For the first time in the course of their acquaintance, she knew he was being completely honest with her and in the process opening up vulnerabilities to her he was not even aware of revealing. That was very precious to Merry, and she could not be angry with him for it.

"And then you start in with your sad stories and your grand principles," he continued with another short breath, "making me care about things that have nothing to do with me, getting me involved in things that are none of my business... Hell, you have me half believing your crazy theories!"

He pushed away from the window, striding toward the door, and Merry watched him with a catch in her heart, not knowing what to say or do. Then, midway across the room, he stopped and turned on her, his eyes dark and his face torn. "Damn it, Merry, you want too much from me! I didn't bargain for this, and I don't want it. I wish I could be the kind of man you need, but I'm not and— Hell, I don't even care!" He came before her, his fingers closing down tight on her arm, his eyes burning darkly into hers. But within those eyes Merry thought she saw more anger at himself than at her, and when he spoke next, she knew it was nothing more than an effort to convince them both of a truth neither believed. "Do you understand that?" he said distinctly. "I *don't care*."

His fingers tightened once, abruptly, before he released her arm, and then he was gone, slamming the door loudly behind him.

When he was gone, Merry sank to the bed

numbly, rubbing her bruised arm, not even feeling the slow track of tears that warmed her cold face.

Now she was truly alone.

Chapter Eight

When Merry passed through the temple gates on Monday she was struck again by that sensation of moving into another world, one that was sealed off by heavy iron gates from all that she knew to be true and right. The smiling faces that moved as in a dream within those gates were trapped there forever between the worlds of fantasy and reality and were so complacent they could not even sense the corruption that tainted every corner of their lives.

It was Merry's moment of truth, her only chance to reach Kevin. From the moment those gates clanged shut behind her, a knot of fear formed in her stomach, for something deep and instinctual told her she did not have a chance of persuading Kevin to leave the cotton-padded world he now called his own for the sometimes-harsh freedom of hers.

Merry had not heard from Mark that day. She hadn't expected to. It was only now, as she parked her car in front of the directory building to which the attendant at the gates had directed her, that she realized how desperately she wished she did not have to go through it alone.

Early that morning she had taken the files back to Maud. She did not feel it was safe to leave them in her room unprotected, and she knew there was nothing more she could do with them. Merry did not want to give up—she would not give up—but for now her first priority was Kevin. And she was not yet ready to admit to herself how dispirited Mark's desertion had left her or how close to home his accusations had hit. Perhaps he was right. Perhaps she should do some serious reevaluation of her motives and her facts before turning her energy toward what could well prove to be no more than a wild-goose chase.

It was a foolish thing, but as long as she had thought he was with her, she felt she could tackle the world. Now that he was gone, she hardly had the impetus to try.

The directory building, which apparently housed the administrative offices, was clean and fresh and air-conditioned, unlike the temple. It could have been any office in the country, except, perhaps, for the fact that it was far more lavishly furnished and that all the workers wore white tunics with a gold symbol woven on the chest.

The reception area was carpeted in powder blue, with blue-and-gold brocaded draperies and wing chairs of French Provincial decor and impressionist watercolors on the walls that Merry knew instinctively were not reproductions. For some reason the opulence of the room reminded Merry of Mark and his decorating binges and that vast empty apartment he came home to every night. And then she had to forcefully push the thought from her mind, because it was threatening to thicken her voice.

The smiling young woman who came forward to greet her welcomed Merry pleasantly, told her she was expected, expressed her joy that Merry had decided to visit them and hoped that should she be inclined to see the rest of the institute she would allow this believer the honor of showing her the way to true enlightenment. Merry swallowed back her distaste and smiled. She had spent the morning preparing herself for it. She would not come to Kevin raging and demanding. She would be calm and understanding and pretend to be open-minded if it killed her. She would meet her brother on his own terms.

The young woman escorted Merry down a corridor toward what she referred to as the "Communion Room," where Kevin would be brought to her. For some reason, Merry did not like the sound of that. She wondered if guards would be posted at the doors and if there would be bars on the windows. To take her mind off the wild flights of her imagination, she asked her escort, "What does it mean—the symbol you all wear on your uniforms?"

The woman touched her shirt lovingly. "The wings are the symbol of perpetual enlightenment. We wear it next to our hearts to remind us that true freedom begins within. Those who have reached the ultimate depth of understanding wear the wings not only on their clothing but in the form of a pendant around their necks, which is never removed. It signifies their closeness to the ideal for which we all strive and, as such, identifies their membership in the Inner Circle of Enlightenment. It is a very great honor that only a chosen few can attain through constant devotion and study."

Merry would have liked to have known more about this "Inner Circle," but just then her escort paused to open the door to a room. "Do, please, be comfortable," she invited. "Would you like some tea while you wait?"

Merry absently agreed that would be nice, but most of her attention was absorbed in the beauty of the room. Even when the door closed gently behind her, she was still a little breathless with it.

It hardly seemed to be a room at all, but more like an island or a cloud world. The walls were covered in sheers of diaphanous curtains that traversed the spectrum of green in graduating degrees, from the palest near white to the deepest jade, drawing focus to a central fountain, lush and verdant, that looked like a waterfall lost in a tropical jungle. On the other side of the fountain the cloudlike curtains began again, going this time from jade to white, forming a circular whole. The carpet was the color of summer grass and just as soft. Around the walls, in hues that blended into the curtains so perfectly they were barely visible, were low benches formed of cushions, and in the center of the room was a round cushioned island that was sectioned into prismatic hues of green.

The entire room was decorated to give the effect of quiet, unearthly isolation. The trickle of the waterfall was tranquil, the cushion of carpet and draperies absorbing excess sound. The colors were soothing but cool. It would be difficult to think harsh thoughts or to express excess emotion in such a room. Merry understood exactly what effect they were striving for and why, but it was nonetheless extremely effective.

The door opened to admit a young woman in white bearing a tray. Merry turned, and their eyes met, but there was nothing in the other woman's face but that customary senseless smile. No sign of recognition, no relief, not even a flash of anxiety.

It was Holly.

Merry came over to her quickly. "Holly!" she exclaimed softly. "I didn't think I'd ever see you again. I'm so glad you were able to get in here. I'm sorry we were interrupted the other day, but I wanted to tell you—"

Holly looked up from pouring the tea with nothing but a slight puzzlement mitigating her smile, and the expression dried up the words in Merry's throat. "Peace upon you, sister," Holly said, "and welcome. They call me Sister Obedience."

Merry scrutinized Holly carefully, an awful, hollow feeling beginning in her stomach. There was no mistake. It was the same person who had stopped her on Saturday afternoon with tears in her eyes, terrified, begging for help. And now there was nothing in her eyes but blank tranquillity, nothing on her face but that expressionless smile. "Don't you remember me?" Merry insisted hoarsely. "Don't you remember—"

Holly handed her a china cup filled with the aroma of peppermint tea. The smile did not waver. "We are all one under the Great Father, sister. I have no memory of life before I came to know the ways of enlightenment, because there was no life before. I would be pleased to tell you how I came to learn the truth if you would care to listen."

For a moment Merry's mind reeled. Holly was not faking. She really didn't remember. In just two days—*two days*—they had done this to her. They had taken a normal, though somewhat frightened, young woman whose only desire was to go home, and they had turned her into this— this zombie of false smiles and preprogrammed phrases in *two days*. Merry felt ill.

The door opened again and was filled immediately with the massive figure of Reverend Samuels. Swathed in the flowing white robes, his only adornment the heavy gold pendant that had come to represent all Merry hated and feared, he looked benevolently from Merry to Holly. And then, in a flicker so quick Merry could very easily have imagined it, she thought she saw a gleam of something very unholy in the man's dark eyes. It looked like cynical amusement. It looked to Merry like a challenge that proclaimed, "There! Do you see what we can do? You with your theories and your principles and your facts and figures—you're helpless against what we can do with the emotions of a young woman in two days."

And Merry was suddenly quite sure that it had all been arranged. Holly had been caught talking to Merry; she had been made an example of. She had been sent to Merry that day deliberately, almost as a warning.

But of course it could have been nothing more than her imagination.

Reverend Samuels touched Holly's head in a kind, dismissive gesture, and the young woman gazed at him worshipfully for a moment before departing. And the reverend turned his absorbing gaze on Merry.

Her cup rattled briefly against the saucer, but Merry could not be certain whether it was from fear or anger. Her chin lifted bravely, and she said quite calmly, "Is something wrong? Am I not going to be allowed to see my brother, after all?"

The reverend smiled, simply, gently. "No, no, my dear." His booming voice, when lowered to a conversational level, was strangely compelling. "He will be along in a moment. I just wanted to welcome you myself and be certain that you were being treated properly."

Bull, Merry thought. *You just wanted to make sure I wasn't causing any trouble.*

But she smiled pleasantly. "Everyone has been most gracious, thank you. Is there a time limit on my visit?"

"No, no, indeed," he assured her with a gracious sweep of his hand. The pendant on his chest caught the muted light and winked sinisterly. "Take as long as you like. Walk around the grounds. Stay and take midday communion with us. We know no time here.''

Merry wondered suddenly and viciously whether the mention of the word ''Astra'' would wipe that complacent smile off the giant's face, but then she forgot about it completely as a figure shadowed the door.

''Kevin,'' Merry whispered.

It was he. It really was. He was thinner. The short-cropped hair made him look different, and there was a strange pale glow to the texture of his skin. But it was Kevin. Her brother. It was he . . . and yet it was not.

He did not wear the tunic of the others she had seen on the grounds and in the temple but a shapeless white robe that covered him from neck to calf, and his feet were bare. Of course, Meredith thought from some faraway part of her brain. What did they call him? A guardian? A monk . . . he never left the temple. He did not need shoes. He never saw the sun. That's why his color was so strange. And his eyes . . . Oh, his eyes. Quiet, blank, perpetually smiling. Not Kevin. Where was Kevin?

While her mind was racing and reeling incoherently, Reverend Samuels smiled at her and said gently, ''Do enjoy your visit.'' Was that a touch of sarcasm she heard in his voice? No, of course not. The great man was beyond such emotions as sarcasm.

Reverend Samuels touched Kevin's arm lightly and left them alone.

Almost half the tea sloshed into her saucer as

Merry placed the cup on the bench. She should have been prepared for it. She was prepared for it. She wasn't going to fall apart. She wasn't going to frighten him away. And she wasn't going to cry.

Kevin stood near the door; Merry stood in the center of the room. She wanted to run the distance that separated them and fling her arms around her brother, but she knew immediately such an action would be inappropriate. She stood there, weakly returning his complacent smile, and then she felt compelled to ask, "Kevin—do you remember me?"

His smile softened. "My name is Brother Light," he responded. "And yes, I know you."

Brother Light, she thought in tightening despair. But she would not let it show on her face. She tried to keep her voice even, her tone pleasant. "It's been a long time." It's been a lifetime. *Damn you, Kevin. It's been a lifetime!* And they stood there, two strangers with half a room separating them, passing inane amenities back and forth.

Kevin made no reply, so she cleared her throat and tried again. "Dad has been really worried about you. We've all missed you at home."

Kevin replied simply. "My earthly father is Reverend Samuels. I have no other."

Then Merry had to turn away. The sudden surge of churning pain and helplessness was almost overwhelming. *What have they done to you? Oh, God, this isn't working. I'll never be able to reach you. I can't even talk to you. . . .*

After a moment, she managed to say, "Do you

think we could sit down?'' Her voice was tight, a little high and not quite even. She would not give up. She had not come that far to give up.

Kevin inclined his head in polite acquiescence, and Merry went to sit on a bench by the wall. Kevin sat at the edge of the waterfall several feet away. "Kevin," she said, folding her hands in her lap. Perhaps if she repeated his name often enough, it would begin to sound familiar to him. He would begin to remember who he was. "Kevin," she said again, "why wouldn't you see Roger when he came last month?"

Kevin's smile was mildly puzzled, not disturbed. "Did he ask to see me?"

It was just as she had thought. They hadn't even told Kevin about Roger's visit. Her determination renewed, she said, "Yes. He made an appointment to see you, and then he was told you didn't want to keep it. They never told you he was here, did they, Kevin? They lied to you."

But her grand thrust had absolutely no effect on Kevin. He merely shook his head, his contented smile deepening with lazy amusement, and he said, "Such unimportant things. Perhaps I forgot."

Merry had to take a deep breath. Apathy, the most difficult condition of all to breach. Even Kevin had learned to rewrite history to suit his own beliefs. How could she fight that? And then the helplessness came seeping through, and she whispered, "Oh, Kevin, how did this happen to you?"

The look he gave her was filled with sympathy

an reproach. "Merry," he said, and her heart jumped when he said her name. He did know her; he did remember. Perhaps there was some hope. But his next words all but crushed that dim possibility. "I don't want you to be unhappy. I want everyone to be as happy as I am. Don't you see," he persuaded gently, "this is my life. This is what I was meant for. I have an inner peace that can't be measured by any standard you know. It's what men seek all over the world but never find because they refuse to look in the only place it ever exists—inside themselves. Merry, I am contented. Please be happy for me."

Merry shook her head slowly, stubbornly, helplessly. "No," she said. "I can't be happy for you when I see you throwing your life away like this. What about all your dreams?" she insisted. "Your ambitions? Kevin, you would have made a fine doctor. It was what you wanted to do and what you were good at. How can you turn your back on it?"

Kevin smiled. "We have a wonderful hospital here. My education is almost completed, and now I heal the spirit as well as the body. This *is* my dream, Merry," he insisted quietly.

"No." She shook her head again in rising agitation mixed with determination, and she got to her feet. "You're living in a fantasy, Kevin," she said tightly, "completely closed off from the real world. You don't know what you're doing. You can't think for yourself. You don't even own yourself anymore! Kevin, can't you see?" She pleaded, coming over to him. "These people— this place—it's all a racket! They take your money, they take your minds, you work for them for nothing. For God's sake, Kevin, look at you! Look at what they've done to you!''

And Kevin was completely unmoved by her outburst. There was nothing in his eyes but a faint pity. "I'm sorry you don't understand, Merry," he said simply. "Nothing would make me happier than to have you come to see the truth yourself, but I'm very much afraid it's too late for you. Your heart is too hard. It saddens me, sister."

Merry stared at him, a cold chill beginning in her stomach that spread all the way up to the nerves of her face. *Too late* ... Too late for Kevin and thousands of others like him, and there was nothing she could do. *Nothing* ...

But she had to try one more time. She had to. She reached out and took his hand. Though he did not flinch from her touch, he did not respond to it, and his skin was very cool. She knelt beside him at the fountain, gentling her features, controlling her voice. "Kevin," she said softly, "do you remember when we were little and the other kids used to pick on you? I always beat them up, because I was the biggest kid on the block, and no one bothered my little brother. Remember?" There was an encouraging softening in his eyes. He did remember. "I even beat you up once or twice," she continued, forcing a note of teasing in her voice. "Even when we were in high school, I could always out arm wrestle you." Meredith felt him slipping away from her again, and her grip on his hand tightened. "Kevin, I still love you," she said intensely. "I still want to protect you. Mom and Dad—they've been sick this past year with worry. We want you back with us. Please come home with me."

And very slowly, very gently, he pulled his hand away. "This is my home, Merry," he said quietly.

For a moment Merry could not speak. She wanted to rage at him. She wanted to take him by the shoulders and shake him; she wanted to grab his arm and drag him forcefully through those gates. She wanted, somehow, to reach inside his mind and *make him see.*

But she had to be calm. She had to think. It was her last chance, and Kevin was slipping further and further away. She forced a very pleasant, very false smile. "For a visit, then," she persuaded. "Just come for a visit. It would mean so much to the folks. They never hear from you, and they do worry." *Just get him out of here,* she thought. *Just get him out of here and we'll work everything else out from there.* "We could take a plane," she suggested quickly, though there was nothing in his face to give her cause for encouragement. "We could be there tonight. Mom would have your favorite dinner ready—you know, lamb chops and braised potatoes and cherry pie for dessert? I'll bet you've missed that! I can almost taste it from here."

Again Kevin's smile was kindly condescending. "We don't corrupt our bodies with meat or sugar," he told her.

"Oh." Merry tried not to let the sudden dip of desperation show. She cast around in her mind frantically. "Well—fresh trout, then. I remember how you used to love it, and no one cooks it like Mom. But the important thing would be to see them, to be home again, just for a little while, Kevin," she pleaded, and even then knew she had lost.

Kevin stood, smiling gently, unmoved. "I wish for you and your parents nothing but happiness," he said quietly. "Please don't concern yourself about me. I have found my way, and I have no regrets."

She knew it then. The boy she once knew as Kevin was sealed deep behind those blank eyes and that smiling face, and there was no way to reach him. None at all. Still, in an automatic reflex, she got to her feet and insisted, quietly desperate, "Just for a visit, Kevin. Just for a little while."

"I will not leave this place," he said simply, finally. "I know no home outside these walls, and I seek no other."

And then, he reached down and pressed her fingers. "Go in peace, sister," he said softly.

And he was gone.

Merry did not know how long she stayed there alone in that room, listening to the trickle of the water and the smothering silence, lost in her own despair. But it seemed like a lifetime.

It was over. Kevin was lost to her, and there was nothing she could do.

But no one had ever told her it would be easy.

Chapter Nine

By the time the sky faded to a twilight blue, Merry had cried all her tears. Over and over she told herself that she had done it wrong; that she had overlooked something, omitted something; that she had said too little or said too much; that the only thing that might have reached Kevin was the one thing she had forgotten to say. She should have been gentler. She should have been more understanding. She should have been stronger, more forceful. She should have been smarter.

She had seen him. That was all she had come there to do. She had talked to him. He was alive and well and completely happy with his life. He did not want to leave.

I'm sorry, Mom, Dad, she thought bleakly. *I tried. I really did. But there was nothing....*

She should have done it better.

She knew she should call her parents. But what would she say to them? That Kevin had been replaced by a blank-faced man who called himself Brother Light and did not acknowledge any father beyond the man Samuels? That their brilliant, shining boy was reduced to an unthinking robot that no amount of parental love could ever reach? That she had tried and had failed?

Merry knew how the mind control worked. Protein starvation, lack of environmental stimulation, constant reinforcement of rote ideals, peer pressure . . . The thinking part of the mind gradually atrophied and was quiescent; new values were substituted for old, and the personality held on to them fiercely, tenaciously. It was a time-honored and indisputably effective method of brainwashing. Nothing could be done to restore the identity until the environment was changed and the long, tortuous road to deprogramming begun. But as long as the victim could not be removed from that environment . . .

Merry knew she would not have another chance. The institute was guarded like a fortress, and the minds of those inside were shielded twice as heavily. She had had her courtesy visit, and now access was closed to her. Kevin would not see her again, even if she should be admitted inside.

And still, far in the back of her mind, those awful doubts lurked. Kevin was happy there. He was worried about nothing, challenged with nothing, protected and secure. He insisted it was what he wanted. Could Mark be right? Did she have the right to interfere in her brother's chosen lifestyle? As long as she had no proof these people were engaged in anything harmful or illegal, where did her moral responsibility end? How could she condemn Kevin for something she did not understand?

She stood at the window, blankly watching the sky darken to navy as the quaint standing-pole streetlights came on and people moved homeward toward their dinners and their families. Stores that did not sell cigarettes or cosmetics. Women who did not wear slacks. Restaurants that did not serve sweets. A whole town . . .

She should go home now. She should go back to her secure, complacent little job, her quiet, self-indulgent life-style, back to her comfortable apartment and Roger's constant nagging and her parents' sad, stoic faces. There was nothing more she could do there.

Meredith thought about driving out to see Maud. Perhaps there was something in those files she had overlooked. No, there was nothing. She had almost gone blind with studying them. She had told Roger about them, and he had not been impressed. Mark had looked at them and seen nothing. She was grasping at straws. There was nothing there. And even if there was, what did she think she could do about it? She, who had never followed through with a project in her life, thought she could take on a multimillion-dollar organization with nothing more than a suspicion and a cause? No, Roger was right. She never should have come there. Mark was right. She was getting involved in things that were none of her business, making mountains out of molehills, seeing shadows in the dark.

She should leave there.

Kevin was lost to her. There was nothing more she could do. She would have to make her parents believe that; she would explain it to them the best she could, and then they would all have to go on living. Somehow Merry would go back to her life and its routine, making happiness the best way she knew how. The past four days would eventually fade into the background, would be forgotten, would be as though they had never been ... Except for one thing.

She told herself she owed Mark the courtesy of saying goodbye. She told herself that the least she could do was apologize and admit to him that he had been right. She knew he did not want to see her. She did not expect him to welcome her with open arms or even to care what she had to say. It even occurred to her that he might be with another woman. But she convinced herself that after all he had done for her, he might want to know the outcome of her meeting with Kevin.

The real reason, of course, was that she simply had to see him one more time.

Meredith washed her face and dilligently reapplied makeup to cover the ravages of the afternoon's tears; then she changed into jeans and a sweater. Mark liked to see her in jeans.

She felt a little better now that she had something definite to do, now that she was out of that room, which had grown heavy with the reminders of her own defeat. On the way to her car she rehearsed what she would say to him. *I just stopped by to tell you I'm leaving. I wanted to apologize for what happened yesterday. I guess I've been pretty much a pain in the neck over this thing, and I just wanted to thank you. Mark, you're the most special thing that's ever happened to me, and it's tearing me apart to just walk out of your life like this, before we even had a chance.*

She was inserting her key into the lock of her car when someone grabbed her from behind. She never heard the footstep, never had a warning. Suddenly, a crushing arm was around her ribs, a tight hand was smothering her mouth, and a body was pressing her thighs into the door handle.

Merry tried to scream, and the bruising fingers tightened on her cheek. She couldn't breathe. Her hands came up to try to pry away the heavy arm that was wedged against her throat but caught only air. Terror was pounding dizziness through her veins, and for a moment everything went dim, then was starkly clear again as a voice hissed in her ear, "You wouldn't take the warning, would you? You thought you were so damn smart!" And the arm tightened once around her ribs, forcing a choked gasp of pain that was strangled in her throat. Her pulses pounded red in her eyes, and her lungs were aching for breath. She was too terrified to even think. "Now you listen to this, lady!" The voice grated. "I don't know what your game is, but it's not going to work! Stay away from us! Go home where you belong!"

He released her so abruptly that she collapsed against the car, grasping at metal that squealed beneath her nails. In a wild and incoherent attempt to regain her balance, she half turned, and it was then that she saw the face of her assailant.

Brother Chi.

The figure melted back into the shadowed park-

ing lot with the same catlike stealth with which it
had emerged, and then Merry's knees collapsed
beneath her; she sank slowly to the hard pave-
ment.

She did not know how long she sat there, shaking and gasping, her knees drawn up to her chest
as though by making herself smaller she could be
a lesser target for something that had already happened. She could still feel the vise of his arm
around her ribs. Her throat ached from the choking pressure he had applied against it, and she
could feel the marks of his fingers on her cheeks,
taste his hand in her mouth. A retching sickness
came upon her, and she fought down bile with the
same mindless strength she choked back sobs—
for no good reason, but because it seemed the
thing to do to keep her terror to herself.

No one had ever attacked Merry before. No
one had ever seriously threatened her or hurt her
in any way. Even her parents had not believed in
spanking. The brutality of the physical assault was
mind-stripping; it was numbing, incomprehensi-
bly frightening.

Her mind was racing—little bits and pieces of
the horror darting back and forth like bats in the
night. What had he said? Stay away... Brother
Chi. He wasn't wearing the uniform. He smoked
cigarettes, and he spied on her in the dark. He had
watched her in the park. Had he scrawled that
message on her mirror? He must have; he said
something about a warning. Why? Why did he
hate her? What had she done? Who was he?

Mark. She wanted Mark. She wanted his strong

arms around her and his cynical little smile telling her to stop exaggerating, his subtly sparking eyes assuring her everything was going to be all right. She had to get to Mark.

There was an endless moment when she could not find her car keys. He could come back. He or someone else could be watching her at that very moment, ready to spring out at her. The parking lot was so dark. Not a sign of life. She could hear the rasp of her own breathing as she frantically swept the asphalt for her keys, grazing her hands and not feeling the pain. The sobs of terror rose up in her throat, and her heart pounded and pounded in her ears so that she couldn't even think. They could be coming back for her, even now.

Her keys were in the lock of her car. Her hand fell upon them disbelievingly, and then she did sob out loud in relief.

Inside her car, the doors locked and the key in the ignition, Merry collapsed with her head on the steering wheel, shaking all over. She couldn't drive. She couldn't even move. All she could do was let the aftermath of shock rack her body and try to force the memory of the hatred in that man's voice out of her mind.

Merry had no clear recollection of how she arrived on Mark's doorstep. The door swung open, and she saw him standing there in wheat-colored jeans and a white sweat shirt, his feet bare and his hair rumpled, as though he had been lying down. She saw and memorized every detail of him: the way the beltless jeans skimmed his waist; the way an errant lock of hair had formed a curl around his ear; the pattern of light hair beneath the pushed-up sleeves of his sweat shirt and a freckle on the back of his hand she had never noticed before; the white scar his recently removed watch had left on his wrist; the shape of his toes; the coarseness of the skin on his neck and the gleam of the gold chain that circumvented the hollow of his throat. There was a very faint ink stain on his index finger. And cautious curiosity, followed by something that might have been alarm, slowly filled his eyes.

Meredith kept herself very calm. Her lips were pressed together, her hands steady on the straps of her purse. And she said, almost evenly, "Could I...come in, please?"

And then she was sitting on the edge of Mark's bed, holding a water glass that was half filled with some brown liquid, and she had no recollection of having got there. Her teeth were chattering, and she was trying very hard to make them stop. Mark's arm was around her shoulders, his other hand cupping hers and urging the glass to her lips. Merry took an automatic sip, tried not to choke and grimaced. Mark's face swam into view through watery eyes.

His smile was gentle and approving, but his eyes looked very worried. "There," he said softly, "that's better. Drink some more."

Merry narrowed her eyes on the glass reluctantly, and he apologized, "It's scotch. I know it should be brandy, but it was the only thing I could find on such short notice. Go ahead." He lifted her hands again. "Drink."

Merry took one more cautious sip, and that seemed to satisfy him. He took the glass from her hands, and Merry said incoherently, "My purse. Did I bring my purse?" Her purse? That was a stupid thing to say. Why had she said that?

Mark assured her soothingly, "Yes, you did. It's in the living room. Do you want it?"

Merry shook her head in embarrassed confusion, looking at him helplessly. "No, I don't know why I said that." Mark's voice was low and reassuring as he bent to lift her feet up onto the bed, propping pillows behind her shoulders. "Here, sit back against the pillows and relax. Sorry the place is such a mess. I was just stretched out here watching TV. I only make my bed once a week, when I change the sheets, which is also the only time the bed is free of cracker crumbs. If you're thinking I live like a pig, you're right; only no one is supposed to know about it." While he talked, simple ordinary words about nonsensical, inconsequential things, he stroked her hair and smiled, gradually orienting her to a sense of time and place and letting her relax in the confidence of his presence. "Now," he continued easily, "what I'm really interested in is what brought you to my door looking like you'd just survived a bad traffic accident and scaring me half to death, so when you get ready to talk about it, please feel free. I only hope," he added with a coaxing smile, "that the look of distress on your face wasn't caused by a sudden overpowering craving for chocolate chip ice cream, because I ate it all, I'm afraid."

Meredith wanted to return his gentle, teasing

smile, but she was afraid if she did she would start crying. She wanted to melt into the warmth of his eyes and sink into the strength of his arms; she wanted to just hold him and let him soothe her and put the entire horrible day behind her. She didn't want to think about any of it, not now, not when she was there with Mark and he was taking care of her.

"I...feel so silly," she managed in a moment. She lowered her eyes, plucking at a fold in the sheet. His sheets were deep pumpkin-colored, with a dark brown stripe. Very bold, very masculine, like Mark. "I guess—" She ventured an uncertain glance at him, for the first time realizing fully what she had done. This man never wanted to see her again; he had made that abundantly clear the night before. Yet she had run to him in time of trouble like a lost child, turning up on his doorstep, distraught and helpless, when he had made it clear he wanted no part of her problems. "I guess," she repeated a little more strongly, "I do look a wreck. I'm sorry, I shouldn't have—"

The tension that suddenly surged through each one of his muscles had been there all along; he had just been keeping it carefully under restraint. But the control within him had reached its limit, and he said tightly, "Darling, I'm sorry, I can't stand it anymore. For God's sake, tell me what happened! Were you in an accident? Are you hurt? Your face is like cotton, and your hair is all messed up, and you're still shaking. Please, what is it?"

She took a breath, trying to fight back the remembered horror that came flooding over her, and she said, "There was a man—"

That was as far as she got. She saw the swift, tight darkening that swept across his features, the coal-fire blaze of his eyes, and he demanded, "Who? Did he hurt you?" His fingers clamped down on her arm, unconscious of their strength. "Who was it, damn it! What did he do?"

Merry shrank back from this shocking display of furious emotion, almost more frightened by the rage in Mark's eyes than she had been by the attack itself. "N-no," she stammered, "he didn't... He just grabbed me, and—and put his hand over my mouth and pushed me against the car, and he said—he said..." With every word the blaze of tightly controlled fury in Mark's eyes deepened, and his hand tightened on her arm until it forced a gasp from her that choked off her words. Abruptly, he released her arm, but he did not say anything. He just kept staring at her with eyes that would bore a hole through her soul, and she forced herself to continue, her voice high and thin, "He said for me to stay away from—from them and to go home. He just grabbed me and...scared me, Mark." The last words were like a plea, and her eyes filled with hot tears again. "That's all!"

Mark got to his feet with such sudden force that the absence of his weight caused the bed to bounce. He took two steps away from her and stood there with his back to her, his arms crossed and his fist doubled against his chin. Straining tension was evident in every line of his back, his rigid neck, the taut, firmly locked muscles of his thighs. She could hear the sharp intake of his breath and then nothing. Silence ticked by like the hands on a clock, and Meredith tried very hard not to cry.

She should not have come there. She should have known better than to come there. Mark wanted no part of her problems. She had no right to come running to him, involving him in her troubles, upsetting him. He was not responsible for her. He wanted no part of it.

Mark said tightly, "Did you see his face? Could you identify him?"

"It was," Merry replied in a very small voice, watching him, "that man... from the park. The one you called Brother Chi."

Mark swore, shortly and viciously, into his closed fist.

He moved abruptly, half turning toward her, and Merry's tightly drawn nerves jumped. Then he changed his mind and swung away toward the window, where he pushed aside the drapery and looked out into the night, pressing his palms against the windowsill, his arms stiff and his back straight in a tense posture of restrained emotion eerily reminiscent of the previous night.

Merry swallowed hard on the tightness of her throat. She was sorry, oh, so sorry, to have come there. She did not want to put Mark through this. What had happened to her was nothing. It wasn't much worse than the warning on the mirror. She hadn't been hurt, just scared. She was making entirely too big a deal out of it, and she had no right to come bursting in there, half-hysterical, crying on Mark's shoulder.

It was just that she was unused to dealing with physical assaults—that was all. It was just that she needed so badly for someone to hold her and comfort her.

Merry pushed herself away from the pillows, swinging her legs over the side of the bed. "I'm sorry," she said. Her voice was small and tight, reflecting everything else within her that was drawn into a hard little ball of self-protection. "I shouldn't have come here. I'll—"

"Stay there!" Mark barked, and that was the final straw. The tears started flowing, and she couldn't stop them. They brimmed over, burning her eyes and scalding her cheeks, and she just sat there, staring at him helplessly, and let them come.

Immediately, Mark was beside her, his face contrite and his eyes filled with pain, his hand touching her hair awkwardly. "Oh, Merry...oh, love..." Slowly, almost hesitantly, he drew her head down onto his shoulder. "Darling, I'm sorry.... It's okay, I know. Cry. Merry, I'm so sorry. It's just when I think of that animal hurting you..." His voice had been hoarse, and there it broke entirely. His arms came around her, very tightly, and he pressed his face to her hair.

Merry held him, clinging to the strength he infused into her, letting him absorb her pain and her fear, letting him take the nightmare of the day and put it to rights again. It was all she had ever wanted, to be held by him.

At last, letting the tears wear themselves out, she turned her face against his sodden shoulder, and she murmured thickly, "I'm being . . . a baby, I know. I'm making too much of it, and I didn't want to scare you. But thanks for being here."

She heard his long, slow intake of breath and felt his chest expand with it. His arms tightened even further, almost desperately, for a brief moment. And then, cautiously aware of the pressure he was exerting against her already bruised ribs, he released her and took her face in his hands.

The defenses were down now. His eyes were open to all his inner agony, his face a study of a man fighting with unfamiliar emotions. And he said huskily, "Merry, those things I said last night—they've been haunting me all day. And then for this to happen..." He took a sharp breath, his lashes lowered and almost closed in the final struggle to subdue an inner pain. When he looked back at her, his eyes were searching hers anxiously, seeking understanding or forgiveness for an unknown crime, or even acceptance. Merry did not know what it was, but she would give it to him, gladly, willingly. All he had to do was ask.

"I didn't mean any of it," he continued at last with difficulty. His voice was soft and husky. "I do care, Merry, more than I ever intended to, far more than I even thought was possible. All day I've been fighting with myself, trying to get up the courage to apologize, knowing that the chances you would just walk out of my life before I ever got the chance. And then..." Again his eyes lowered, and so did the pitch of his voice. "Thinking it might be better if you did." Then, quickly, before she could say anything, he looked back at her again. "But it wasn't," he admitted softly. "I'm so glad you came here tonight, Merry, that you're safe, that I can hold you."

And he did. They blended together into one fierce embrace of shared need and weakening relief, and Merry felt all of her fears, all her disappointment and her failure and her hurt, melt into the quiet, simple joy of him. *If nothing else,* she thought quietly, intensely, *if nothing else, I have him. For as long as it lasts.*

They were lying back against the pillows, his hand warm and firm upon her back beneath the sweater, her hands linked around his bare waist where his sweat shirt rode up above the jeans. The feel of his flesh against her palms was hypnotically soothing; just that simple touch was enough to drive away the demons and make her feel secure. She wanted to stay like that, locked in his arms, forever.

Then he moaned softly against her neck. His hand moved over her back restlessly, and he lifted his face to look at her. "Now see what I'm doing," he said. There was a hint of shame and self-contempt in his eyes. "I still want to make love to you." And he started to move away.

Merry caught his hand. Her eyes were quiet, filled with the simplicity of her need. "Is there something wrong with that?" she whispered.

Mark looked at her for a moment, questioning,

disbelieving, hesitant. "After what you've been through..." he began haltingly.

Merry shook her head slowly against the pillows, her hair forming a rippling aura around her face as she did. The movement of light and shadow seemed to fascinate Mark as much as the implications of the gesture did; she watched his pupils widen with it. "After what I've been through," she said softly, "I need you, that's all. Hold me, Mark. Love me. Make me feel strong again."

His eyes closed slowly with the helpless onslaught of emotions as his lips descended upon hers. She drank of his kiss as he did of hers, and she felt her soul opening to him like a thirsty bud unfolding to the rain. Simple, unmitigated joy filled her, a growing peace that had the power to overcome any obstacle. Nothing could harm her, nothing could frighten her, nothing too much for her, as long as he was by her side.

His hands moved beneath her sweater, pushing it upward; light nibbling kisses covered the expanse of abdomen that was revealed. Beneath the heavy, mind-drowning languor that filled her, Meredith murmured lazily, "Mark, there's just one thing."

His face came up; he placed a light brushing kiss across her cheekbone and then her forehead. The smile in his eyes was brilliant. "Anything, love."

Meredith's lips tightened with a smile that was half-teasing, half-shy. "I don't...look as good without my clothes as I do with them. Could we turn off the light?"

Mark started to chuckle, and then he began to

laugh. His eyes snapped with it, his whole face glowed with it, and it spread through Merry like diamond-sparkled sunshine. "Darling," he exclaimed, "you are priceless! And every inch of your body, with or without clothes, is like gold to me. But..." He reached forward and turned the lamp switch, suffusing the room in a misty blue darkness. "Tonight, and for you..."

He turned back to her, and the easy, silvery, rich mood slowly began to sober. He sat above her, his hands stroking her face, studying her intensely in the dark with his eyes and his mind and his touch, as though trying to memorize with unfamiliar senses all that he knew about her already.

Merry's hands rested on his forearms, and she looked up at his shadowy figure, her eyes glowing with so much contented admiration that she thought they must surely be a beacon that could penetrate the darkest night. She could feel it building within him, this quiet influx of wonder and cautious joy, as though it were a tangible thing that flowed between them. His hands moved over and over her face, smoothing brow and cheekbones, rhythmically and hypnotically, and his eyes never moved from hers. And then, just before he brought his face down to rest against hers, he drew a sharp, low breath. He whispered, "God help me, Merry. I think I'm falling in love with you."

And it was love they shared and created in that timeless interval of wordless communication. It blossomed between them, and it enfolded them; it penetrated the deepest core of each of them and left its life-force behind. They moved together in silent harmony, just as each of them had always known they would. Lips touched and fingers caressed; hands linked and legs embraced. They knew the taste and the scent and the feel of each other, the pulse and the breath of each other. They knew each other's minds, the strength and weaknesses, the tenderness and the demands. Restraints were left behind and gateways unbarred as they gave of themselves selflessly and took selfishly. No mysteries stood between them and no caution made them wise as each of them opened to the other all they had to give, offering easy access to their most secret souls.

They lay curled together at last, his legs sheltering hers, her body tucked into the strong length of his, his arms holding her and her hands, moving almost without direction from her mind, caressing him. She felt again the lean sculpted muscle of his arm and the shoulders that had strained with holding her only moments before. Now those muscles were relaxed and quiescent, but with an undercurrent of alertness that sent a new shiver of awareness through Merry. Her fingers were compelled to renew acquaintance with those parts of him that had been too little explored during the concentrated urgency of lovemaking. She traced the shape of his ear and the funny little curl that curved around it; she felt his smile in the dark. She touched with wonder the lips that had created such magic within her, whose gentle upward curve still had the power to make her weak. She explored the sensitive hollow of his throat, and her fingers absently followed the circle of gold chain around his neck until it ended in a medallion at his chest. Yet within the warm glow of remembered passion and seeping contentment, certain unavoidable truths began to merge. Mark was very quiet, and Merry wondered if he was thinking the same thing she was.

Nothing was fundamentally changed between them. In a moment of desperation and need, they had each acted upon the impulse for self-gratification, and it had been all they had expected, and more. Yet now that the passion was sated, the problems that had confronted them had not magically disappeared; they were, in fact, more visible than ever. Merry wanted it to last forever, but she had a life waiting for her four states away, and there was no more reason to stay there. That night she had been attacked and viciously warned to leave this place, and though the horror of the scene faded beneath the shelter of Mark's arms, it was something that had yet to be dealt with.

Mark had said he was falling in love with her. What did that mean? What did it change? Would he fight her battles for her? Would he take up a cause he did not believe in because she had lain in his arms in one moment of miracle-working passion and desperate fulfillment? Mark did not have long-term relationships. He did not get involved; he did not care. But he had cared for her that night, hadn't he?

Mark bent his head and placed a tender kiss upon her temple. He did not know what to say, either. It was too soon for him to say anything. Merry wondered what would happen if she told him now that this was goodbye, that she would be going home the following day.

She sighed and folded herself close to him, her hand moving upward again to caress his neck. "Oh, Mark," she whispered, "why can't things ever be easy?"

His arm tightened around her briefly. "I don't know, love," he answered heavily. "I really don't."

Again her fingers trailed down the length of the gold chain, closing around the decoration at the end, absently caressing its shape. She lay in the warmth of Mark's arms, her mind weighted with unwanted thoughts. It took a long time for the sensation of familiarity her fingers noted to register. And even a longer time for Meredith to believe it.

The shape of the pendant beneath her fingers was smooth and elliptical, intersected in the middle by a free-sculpted shape, like wings. Her heart began to pound with slow, painful clarity, and in response she felt Mark's muscles tense. Hesitantly, horribly, she retraced the symbol with her fingers.

There was no mistake. A smooth elliptical outline, its centre formed by two intersecting V's.

It was the sacred emblem of the Source of Enlightenment.

Chapter Ten

Merry sat up slowly, as in a dream, and reached for the lamp switch. The bright yellow glow cast everything into stark relief, and for a moment there was a sense of disorientation, as though she had awakened from a nightmare to find it was real or as though she had stepped over a familiar threshold to find nothing but a sheer drop beneath her feet. Mark's face, the rapid blinking of his eyes in the sudden light, unable to disguise his alarm; the shape of his chest, that beautiful chest that only moments earlier had lain against hers in intimacy; muscles now tightening in defense as he sat up. Their clothes, scattered in obscene array around the bed. The rumpled pillows. The forgotten glass of scotch on the nightstand. And that pendant, seeming to take on a life and glow of its own as it winked and glittered against his chest. That symbol of evil and corruption, a brand of ownership upon its wearer. It stared at her, it beckoned her, it mocked her; it caught sparks of light and threw them back to her in hypnotic waves, and over and over again her mind echoed,

No. No, Mark, it's not true. There's an explanation. Tell me it's not true, Mark.

Mark said nothing.

What was it the woman had said about the pendants? Merry's mind was spinning; she couldn't think. What was that peculiar pounding sound? Why did her chest hurt so? *Constant devotion and study... Worn next to the heart and never removed... Inner Circle of Enlightenment... Chosen few...* And within her head a scream was building that seemed to well up from the center of her abdomen, *Mark... Not Mark...*

Mark started to reach for her, and the movement snapped her out of the frozen spell. She jerked away, started to run, then realized she was naked. Frantically, she scrambled amid the tangled covers and on the floor for her clothes and came up with Mark's sweat shirt and her own underpants, and she screamed hoarsely at him, "For God's sake, where are my clothes?"

Mark moved quickly, stepping into his jeans as he got out of bed, gathering up the remainder of her clothes while she sat, drawing the sheet tightly around her, trying to push away the numbing horror and thinking only about getting out of there, of fleeing the taint of contamination and betrayal that pressed down on her from every corner of the room.

"Don't look at me!" she commanded as she took her clothes from him, and one look at her wild eyes and the raw pain of her face caused Mark to avert his face, then to cross to the other side of the bed.

"For God's sake, Merry, if you'd just listen..."

His voice was hoarse and strained, but it did nothing to calm the shaking pulse of horror that repeatedly assaulted Merry from the inside out. She pulled her sweater over her head and tugged on her jeans, but even then she did not feel fully clothed or adequately protected. The profane act she had just performed with the monster who was her lover and left her stripped in ways that could never be recovered.

She sat down again to pull on her shoes, and then he was beside her, grasping her arm. She jerked away, and her hand came up wildly to strike, but he caught it in midair. For a moment she struggled, and the fight showed in the grimness of his face as well as the fury and fear in hers, but his superior strength won out. He pushed her arm with a snap back onto the bed, not releasing it. "Now listen to me," he commanded. He was breathing hard, and droplets of perspiration were beginning to dampen the strands of hair that fell onto his forehead. His eyes were dark and determined, but beyond them she thought she caught a hint of desperation, and that was his weakness. "You're flying off the deep end over nothing! It's not—"

"You lied to me!" she screamed at him. "You were on their side all along! You—"

"Damn it, Merry, it doesn't matter! It has nothing to do with sides. It's not—"

"Let me go!" She struggled violently to free her arm, and both of his hands came up to clamp

down on her shoulders, pressing her back against
the headboard, holding her firm.

"No!" he said. His white, anger-filled face was
close to hers. "Not until you calm down and discuss this thing with me intelligently."

And suddenly all the rage, all the fear and
the shock, drained away into pain; a low, slow-
moving, excruciating pain that moved from the
center of her upward, blotting out everything in
its path. She closed her eyes against it; her face
started to crumple with it, and she thought, *No.
Not Mark. Oh, please, God, no. Make him say something, anything to convince me it's not true. Make me
believe him. Don't let this happen.*

Mark's grip upon her shoulders gradually lightened as he felt the tension draining from her
muscles. Discuss it, he had said. She wanted to
discuss it. She wanted to know every hateful detail. She wanted to know how he had used her and
trapped her and laughed at her, how he had plotted to seduce her to gain her good favor and make
her give up the fight. She wanted him to tell her
she was wrong, that it was all a mistake; that he
really wasn't a part of the force that had destroyed
her brother's life and so many others; that he
wasn't behind everything she had been fighting
since coming there; that he hadn't deceived her or
betrayed her and that the past ten minutes had
been only a bad dream.

And in the end she said tiredly, dully, "There's
nothing to discuss." She looked at him with quiet,
blank eyes and allowed not the faintest shred of

hope to seep through. "You are a part of the organization, aren't you?"

For the longest time he didn't answer. Then he dropped his eyes. "Yes," he said quietly. And he looked at her again. "I'm the financial manager for the Stonington headquarters."

It hit her like a blow to the stomach, a low, breathtaking pain, and then there was nothing. Financial manager. She should have guessed. She should have known all along. It was so obvious.

She said, without any emotion at all. "We didn't meet by accident that night in the lounge. You were waiting for me. You knew all about me. You knew where I was from and when I had arrived and what I was doing there. But what was the point?" she inquired with only the slightest edge of real curiosity. It hardly mattered now. "What were you planning to do—kidnap me? Dazzle me with your charm so that I would forget the whole thing and go home? What?"

A grim line appeared near Mark's mouth, and he at least had the good grace to drop his eyes. "I wasn't supposed to do anything," he replied tiredly. "Since I was the one closest to the hotel, I'm the one they called when you arrived. I was just supposed to check you out, that's all."

The one, she thought. *The one of what?* And then the answer presented itself calmly: the Inner Circle, of course. The chosen few. *Constant study and devotion . . .*

"But you didn't try to stop me," she pointed out. "You even took me out there."

"There was no reason to stop you," he answered simply. "All you wanted was to see your brother. You weren't a trained deprogrammer ready to storm the place and take him out. It was decided it would be best if you were allowed to go about your business without interference."

She liked the way he put that. It was decided. Not *they* decided or *we* decided. Professional deceiver to the end, he was still being very careful.

"But what about the warning on my mirror?" she reminded him, her voice even and detached.

His eyes jerked up to hers with instant denial. "I had nothing to do with that," he insisted sharply.

Meredith's lips found a dry half curve that did not touch her voice or her eyes. "Unauthorized intervention, huh?"

His eyes flashed quick anger mixed with hurt, but she continued calmly. "And what about Holly? I told you about her. You turned her in, and they did something to her—"

"No!" he denied quickly. "I don't know anything—"

But she went on tonelessly, "You had me fooled, Mark. You surely did. An award-winning performance." And she tilted her head to the side in a posture of objective scrutinization. "You don't look like them," she observed. "Long hair, street clothes... Where's your little white shirt?"

She could see each of her words pinning him down like separate arrows, and he did not know how to squirm away. He took a breath. "We—certain people—are only required to put up the front for the kids at the temple," he answered her uncomfortably. But his eyes met hers without flinching. She had to give him credit for obstinacy, if nothing else. "The rest of the time we're just like—"

"Any guy on the street," she supplied tonelessly. They drank vodka, they wore street clothes, they smoked cigarettes. Sometimes they lurked in shadows, watching. Sometimes they sprang out of the dark to attack. "Long hair, gold watch, tailored clothes," she continued softly. "A flask in your pocket, enough charm to choke a horse. No, you weren't exactly what you appeared to be. Just like your friend Brother Chi." Mark's eyes sharpened as he sensed it coming, but Meredith demanded, anyway, very calmly, "Was it your idea tonight, Mark? Did you set him on me? If so, your information was a little outdated, because I was ready to go home, anyway."

"No!" He sprang to his feet, a sudden fierceness darkening his face. "I had nothing to do with that. I— Good God!" he exclaimed hoarsely, and the raw pain on his face almost convinced her. Almost. "Do you really think I'd try to hurt you? That I'd let someone else . . ."

Merry hardened herself against the incredulity and the horror in his eyes. "I don't know, Mark," she said softly. "Would you?"

"Damn it, Merry. Don't you understand what I've been trying to tell you?" He took an abrupt step from her, his fists balled at his sides in furious impotence; then he swung back. "It's all a sham! This—" He gave a hateful swipe with his open hand at the pendant against his chest. "This whole Inner Circle garbage—it's just an act! I don't give a damn what goes on with those people. I'm not a believer. I just handle their damn money! What do I care whether your brother stays or goes? It has nothing to do with me—or with Samuels himself, for that matter! We're just in it for the money!"

He knew immediately, of course, that it was the wrong thing to say, and he closed his eyes with a soft oath of defeat and turned away. But it flowed over Meredith without surprise. She thought about Kevin, quietly and blindly devoted to a cause that did not even exist. She thought about Holly as she had been two days before, and Holly as she was now. She thought about a town populated with blank smiling faces and restaurants that didn't sell sweets. She thought about Maud's husband and an "accidental" fire. For the money. Of course.

And then Mark said harshly. "All right. I tried to tell you all that before. It's just a business like any other, no worse than some I've dealt with and a lot better than others. I never claimed to be a saint, Merry, but I swear to you," he said intensely, taking a step toward her, "I never did anything or knew about anything that could hurt you."

Merry bent down slowly and began to pull on her shoes. Oh, no. He had never pretended to be a saint—perhaps the only thing he had not pretended to be. *I am a man totally without scruples.* She almost smiled at that. He had tried to tell her. Yes, he had.

She stood up slowly, her face perfectly expressionless, and Mark took a half step toward her, then was still. "Merry," he said quietly, "listen to me. I can work with you. If something really is going on at the institute that shouldn't be—if there was something behind that attack tonight besides just one crazy man—then we can find it out together. I can help you," he persuaded, his eyes softening with a near plea. "I'm on the inside. I have access to information you don't. I'm on your side, Merry."

Oh, how easy it would be to believe him. How much she wanted just to sink into his arms and let him protect her. And the sudden sharpening need was like a knife wound to her solar plexus. Why, when all else was dead, wouldn't the love go away?

You'd be a fool to trust me.

Merry started to move past him.

Mark caught her arm, his face tightening with subdued desperation, his eyes a dark turmoil. "Don't do this, Merry," he said, and his voice was a hoarse half whisper. "Don't do it to us—to me." And he stepped in front of her, grasping her upper arms, and the fear and the pain she saw in his eyes was almost too much for her to bear.

"You're the only thing I've ever cared about in my life," he said. "Don't take it away from me now—not like this!"

What she saw in his eyes was so desperate, so sincere and so forceful that she had to fight with everything she had to resist it. For a moment it was as though none of it had ever happened. For a moment he was only the man she loved, and she was hurting him, and all she wanted to do was put her arms around him and make the hurt go away.

He saw the weakening in her eyes and a flash of hope leaped into his, but then, forcefully, with all the will she possessed, Merry closed the shutter on her heart. She pulled away from him very slowly, and he let her go.

When Mark heard the door close behind her, he sank to the bed, his face in his hands, breathing heavily. He stayed like that for a long time.

Chapter Eleven

Merry smiled and inclined her head in greeting toward the young man in the white tunic who passed, keeping the file folders high upon her left breast. His eyes registered nothing but blank complacency as he moved on down the corridor, and her heart started beating again. There was no other sound in the climate-controlled hallway, no hint of approaching footsteps, no rustle of material, no sonorous voices. But still Merry strained to listen, not moving. These people moved like cats, and she could not be too careful.

Careful. The word struck a hilarious chord in her, and the sound almost made it to her throat. Insane, perhaps; hysterical, quite possibly; but careful. Her actions at the moment were far from it.

She wondered which of the frosted-door offices that lined the corridor was Mark's.

It had taken until dawn for Merry to make the decision, if it could even be properly called that. The night had passed timelessly, sleeplessly and, strangely, with very little emotion. It was as though the shock of Mark's betrayal had torn a hole in the fabric of illusion that had protected Merry all her life, allowing her to see clearly for the first time.

Mark had been right about one thing. She had taken on the project for a selfish reason that she had idealized to suit her purpose. She wanted to be a heroine to her parents, to impress them and herself with her levelheadedness and strength of purpose; there had been nothing noble about her motivations at all. She had been unable to return triumphant with Kevin at her side, and she had been ready to turn her back on her mission when all the glory had gone with nothing more than a "nice try" for consolation. All the time her heart and not her head had ruled her actions, and she had overlooked—willingly—some pretty important facts. The ease of Mark's deception was proof of that.

But in the cold, clear hours of dawn, all those facts marched together with definitive purpose and took on a solid and unrelenting shape. She could not reach Kevin, not by herself and not in the traditional way. She had to accept that. But something larger was going on there; her intuition had warned her of it from the moment she walked into town, and logic had been shouting it at her at various intervals throughout her stay. She had just been too self-absorbed, and perhaps too lazy, to dedicate her full attention to it. But no more. This was one job she was not going to walk out on before it was finished.

There were two indisputable pieces of evidence

she could no longer push aside: a young woman experiences a complete personality change in two days. She goes from a terrified, pleading and very vulnerable spirit to a bland, smiling, totally content young woman—with an apparent memory loss. Even the most sophisticated methods of brainwashing could not accomplish that result in such a short time. There had been nothing fake about Holly's behavior on either occasion; something had been done to alter her personality. Something drastic, perhaps violent, in all likelihood illegal. That was cause enough for investigation.

But there was still the matter of Maud's husband's theories. She had almost let Roger, then Mark, talk her out of attaching any real significance to them. She had almost been ready to abandon the investigation as foolish and futile. What Jonathan had been on to Merry did not know—if, indeed, there was anything at all to his suspicions. But she did know that anything that had to be filtered through dummy corporations was hardly likely to be legal, and all she needed was some proof, no matter how small, that could cast a genuine shadow of suspicion upon the organization to give her the ammunition to begin a full-scale investigation.

She might be wrong. She might fail. But it was one thing she had to prove to herself that she could pursue. Because this time, this one and only time, she knew it was the right thing to do. Not the selfish thing, certainly not the easiest thing, but the right thing.

Her methods were drastic and almost laughably naive, and later Merry would wonder how she ever found the courage to attempt such a crazy scheme. It might have been the long night of sleeplessness. It might have been the shock of the traumatic events of the preceding twenty-four hours. Or it might have been pure foolishness. But at the time the procedure seemed very clear: she needed to find out what they had done to Holly, and she had to have some proof of foul dealings on the corporate level. And the only way she was going to get either of those things was by first gaining access to their fortress.

At nine o'clock she called, and pretending to be her mother, asked to speak to Reverend Samuels. She was told he would be out of the compound until three in the afternoon. That was luck. It could be done that day.

At nine-thirty she called to make an appointment with Mark. That was playing the odds, and she was prepared for it either way. If Mark was in, she knew he would see her. Curiosity, if nothing else, would compel him. And once inside his office, she could deal with him. After all, hadn't he begged her to allow him to help the night before? Of course it was all a lie, and of course she would never trust him, but Mark did not have to know that. If nothing else, Mark had taught her a thing or two about deception. She would play him for all he was worth, if she had to.

But she didn't have to. The secretary told her that he was not expected in that day, and Merry wasn't particularly surprised. The shock of his discovery would have upset quite a few of his plans; he would need some time to regroup. At that point, Merry pretended to be regretful and confused and told the secretary that Mark had promised he would deliver a letter to her brother if she brought it by his office, and as she was leaving that day, she really didn't know what to do. The secretary, of course, ever obliging, as they all were trained to be, invited Merry to come by and leave the letter with her. That was how she got inside the administrative building.

Dressed in a white smock that she had purchased when the stores opened that morning, wearing no makeup, Merry had waited until the secretary left her desk to deliver, at Merry's soulful request, the letter to Mark's desk personally. Then she grabbed a handful of file folders from the top of the desk and followed the directory down the hall toward Reverend Samuels's office.

She had to duck into a niche that hid the water fountain when the secretary came back up the hall, but no one else gave the young woman with long flowing hair and a white dress a second glance. She was careful to keep the folders over the place on her dress the gold symbol should be, her smile constant and her pace sedate. She looked like any one of the dozens of other office workers in the building. Reverend Samuels's door was clearly marked, and she found it with no trouble. Now, if only it wasn't locked...

It wasn't. Her slightly damp palm closed around the doorknob, and it turned. She couldn't believe it. Her heart started to pound, more loudly than before, and her throat felt dry. This was spooky. It was crazy even to try such a thing; it was stupid. And it was entirely too easy.

She closed the door behind her and leaned against it for a long moment, trying to breathe evenly. The room was lit only by a skylight, and it was cloudy that day, shrouding the room in a misty dimness. But it was better that way. She wouldn't dare turn on a lamp, and no one would see her shape moving behind the frosted door window.

It was crazy. The thought struck her again. She had never expected to get that far. Why would such a place leave the door to their chief executive's office unlocked when he was away?

Perhaps he wasn't away. Perhaps it was all a trap, a neatly plotted scheme to get her inside where they could deal with her. A dozen bizarre explanations flashed through her head, and only the strength of her newfound common sense dismissed them. *Logic,* she told herself firmly. *Logic.* The only doors that were kept unlocked were those that protected nothing of value. She had come to that office because she thought, if anywhere, incriminating records would most likely be kept there. But obviously not. If there was anything important there, she would not have been able to get in so easily.

The room was as elegant as any penthouse office she had ever visited, but Merry was little concerned with the details. Quickly, she went over to a long row of mahogany files, trying the drawers on reflex. Locked. The credenza was also locked. The Venetian-glass-enclosed bookcase was not locked, but there was nothing to interest her there. There was a bathroom, opulent and empty, and a closet with nothing but an umbrella stand. If there was anything helpful there, it was most likely hidden in the files or the locked credenza. Did she dare try to break in? And if so, how?

With her mind still racing with those problems, she sat down at the huge mahogany desk and absently tried the center drawer. To her great surprise, it slid open easily.

And spilling out across two file folders and a scattering of other loose papers, almost jumping up at her, were a dozen black-and-white snapshots of herself.

The sensation was for the very briefest of moments almost like staring at her own corpse. It caused a chill of shock and distaste to go over her, a sense of invasion and accusation to see her own face looking back at her, unaware: sitting in the hotel dining room, walking down the street, laughing up at someone, in the park, in her own hotel room, looking out the window. She made herself touch them. She made herself pick each one of them up and look at them, and then something odd and most disquieting occurred to her. Mark had not taken those pictures. When first she saw them, she assumed he had, that it had been his job all along to spy on her, to keep tabs on her. But Mark was in one of the pictures in the park, his face blurred in movement as he turned to look at her, and something soft and painful started to flow through her as she saw that face, that familiar figure—Mark.

Swift reason came back. No Mark had not taken the pictures. It was his friend Brother Chi. All Mark had to do was set her up; he did not have to be involved in any of the dirty work. Impatiently, smothering distracting anger, Merry brushed the pictures aside and picked up the two folders beneath them. The first one had her brother's name on it, but she did not pause to consider the significance of that, because the second one was—

"Oh, my God." It was whispered out loud, and Merry stared at the label on the folder in numb, disbelieving shock. In neatly typed letters it said, "Astra."

She had to close her eyes for a moment, unable to comprehend her luck. He had left the file lying around in an unlocked drawer—the very project Jonathan had been so excited about, the project that dealt with the stock market and possible illegal activity. No, he wouldn't have done that. He wouldn't be so careless. It was not the right file. There was nothing of a damaging nature inside it. If there was, it would have been more closely guarded.

But then it came to her simply, easily. Why should anything be guarded inside this building? Reverend Samuels had the complete loyalty of mindless robots who would not recognize a wrong-doing if they saw it. These people were completely under his control. He had no need to protect himself from anything. Oh, they were very careful to keep strangers out, but once inside the compound, all their people could be trusted; their secrets were accessible, because they had grown complacent in their power. And that was their big mistake.

Merry opened the folder and quickly scanned the pages in the dim light. She was accustomed to reading complicated documents, and it did not take her very long to put together a picture from this one. It was all too horrifyingly clear. The Middle East. *Oil.*

From what little she knew of the oil market, Meredith could guess that the Source of Enlightenment, through various corporations under a multitude of names, was well on its way to controlling a major share of the world's natural fuel deposits. Their holdings in the Middle East were strong enough to give them prominent influence with the OPEC nations—enough power, at least, to start a good-sized war.

But the story grew grimmer. Dating back two years earlier, the report methodically listed the acquisition through various corporations of huge amounts of refined oil, its sale to other corporations within the Astra network, its shipment and its storage. Meredith had to check her conclusions twice, and her heart was pounding so hard with excitement that she could barely read the figures. But there was no mistake. It was a complete record of the carefully planned Astra project; acquisition, shipment, storage—but no distribution. They were stockpiling oil.

Not stocks, Mark had said. *Commodities.*

Meredith sat back, suddenly calm as it all came

together for her. Oil, perhaps the most precious commodity of all. They were hoarding it, and they had been doing so over a period of years quietly and unobtrusively, keeping the market price relatively stable, until now they were ready to, as the final report indicated, "move aggressively in the international marketplace." They were manipulating the world economy in the most dangerous fashion conceivable, with the one commodity nations had been ready to go to war over for years, and when they decided to declare a shortage, they could set any price they wished.

The oil crisis of the mid-seventies would be nothing compared to what they had planned. And it would all be so devastatingly simple. All they had to do was stir up a little trouble in the Middle East, declare a crucial shortage, watch the gas lines form and the riots in the streets begin ... and rake in the profit. Only this time perhaps the situation would not be resolved quite as easily as it had been during the last oil crisis. This time there was an enormously powerful political and financial network manipulating it all, and the fates of nations were involved.

This time there might be no way to avert global war.

It was all like something out of a futuristic thriller. It was inconceivable. It was diabolical; it was horrifyingly brilliant. And it was all there in black and white. They were really doing it.

Quickly, Merry closed the drawer and stuffed the Astra file in the midst of the blank folders she had carried in there. Her hands were shaking, and she almost dropped it. She had her proof now. No one would turn a blind eye to manipulation of the oil market. No amount of power in the world would protect them from prosecution now.

She hurried around the desk, intent upon the door, and her heart was pounding so erratically against her ribs it hurt to move. She had no idea how she was going to get out carrying the folder. But she had gotten in.

And then the door swung open, and Brother Chi filled the threshold. Merry froze.

Too easy, she thought, dully and from far away. *I knew it was too damn easy.*

For a long moment they stared at each other, everything within Merry still and silent and coiled with anticipation. He had worked hard to keep her away from there. He had outdone himself to make certain she did not discover their secrets. And now that she had them, what would he do?

Brother Chi said sadly, "You just wouldn't listen, would you?"

Merry did not move. He took a step toward her, his eyes dark and calm, and she couldn't even think.

"I tried to keep you out of the way," he continued, still approaching at his own stealthy pace, "but you're one stubborn broad. I hate to do this, lady, but I can't have you coming in here screwing everything up, not when we've waited so long."

She saw his hand lift for her, and in the flash of a second she thought of a dozen possibilities, a cornucopia of scenarios. She thought about flinging the files in his face and running. She thought about trying to overpower him. She thought about Mark.

"Well, what a surprise. I didn't know anyone was in here."

Brother Chi was about two feet away from her, his hand descending to grab her arm. The voice came from the doorway behind him, and the relief that swept through Merry was so overpowering it blinded her; her knees went weak, and she thought for moment she might actually collapse. If there was anything familiar about the voice, it did not register.

She saw the sharp tightening of Brother Chi's face, the dark flash of anger and indecision. But it lasted only a second before he turned away from her gracefully, the smooth mask already on his face. He inclined his hand toward the figure by the door and slipped easily past.

The man approached her, and Merry stared.

Perspiration was gathering around her eyes, and she could not be sure she saw clearly. She blinked rapidly, but he was still there. The file slipped from her numb fingers and scattered on the floor. Not a dream, not a mirage. It was really he.

"Roger," she whispered, and then her knees gave way; she collapsed weakly against the desk.

Swiftly, he was beside her, his hands fastening under her armpits, moving her to the chair. "Whoa, girl, take it easy," he said. "You look like you've seen a ghost. What did that guy do to you?"

Roger. Dear, competent Roger, with his receding hairline and his slight paunch, dressed so correctly in the three-piece suit, smelling of English Leather and starch. It was really he. She did not know why he was there, how he had found her, what had brought him into that room at precisely the right minute, but at the moment she didn't care. He was there.

"Oh, God, Roger," she whispered weakly, and she buried her face in her hands. For the moment she could do nothing but sit there and let the tremors of shock and relief overtake her, trying to catch her breath, trying to make her heart stop pounding, trying to make herself believe that she had been rescued at the last moment by a knight in shining armor.

Roger patted her head awkwardly and murmured soothingly, "There, there." He obviously didn't know what else to do with her. It was so typical of Roger that she wanted to smile. He was a breath from home. He was real and good, and he had come to save her, and for the time that was all that mattered.

Her strength returned, and she sat up with a breath. Roger looked at her worriedly. "Are you okay now? What were you doing in here, anyway? What's this?"

He bent to pick up the folders, and Merry's story came rushing out in such a desperate flow that she did not even notice the changing expressions on his face as he picked up the papers. "Roger, that's it," she said breathlessly. "That's the proof we need to close this place down. They're manipulating the oil market, Roger. They've been stockpiling oil, and they're planning to declare a shortage and a price hike like you wouldn't believe. Thank God you got here! We've got to get those papers out of here. We've got to get a court order for the rest of their records."

Very slowly, Roger turned around, arranging the papers in their folder, and his face was oddly expressionless. "Now, Merry," he said calmly, "don't go running off out of control. Just calm down, take a deep breath, get yourself together." The smile he gave her incredulously staring face was forced, and he spoke as though to a child. "What in the world do you know about oil?" he insisted gently. "Obviously, you're off on another one of your crazy tangents. This is a serious charge, Merry. You can't just—"

"Are you *crazy*?" She leaped from the chair, urgency and frustration igniting impatient anger in her. "Look for yourself— No, not now. We have to get those papers out of here; then you can be as pedantic as you please. You can go over it with every fine-tooth comb you can find, but don't you know what they'll do to us if they find us here?"

And Roger merely smiled at her. "Do you?" he asked quietly, and with a very gentle pressure on her shoulder, he pushed her back down into the chair.

Something cold and clammy seeped through Merry. She looked at him, smiling at her calmly, regarding her with complacent pity, and she could not believe it, could not understand it. "What—"

she managed hoarsely through dry lips. "What are you doing here?"

He tilted his head at her as though that was an enormously stupid question. "Why, I came to help you, of course. You didn't really think I'd let you get into something like this by yourself, did you? I knew you'd only find trouble."

A low dark, ugly certainty began to boil in her stomach, to assault her with waves of horror, to shoot in streams of panic through her veins, yet still she was able to speak, still she could demand. "How did you get in here? How can you just walk in this place and stroll back to Samuels's office? You knew I was here. They told you I was here, just like they told Chi—"

She sprang from the chair, and his hands were on her shoulders swiftly and ruthlessly, pushing her back and holding her there. His eyes were dark, and his face was tight, but his voice was very calm. "You're far too excited, Merry," he soothed. "I think you must be headed for a breakdown. All this stress—you need a long rest."

Abruptly, his hand moved to bear down hard on the center of her chest, near her throat, while the other hand reached for the telephone. But he had no need to hold her. Merry could not have moved at that moment had she the chance.

He punched a single button on the telephone and spoke into it pleasantly. "Would you send Brother Light up here with his bag? One of our—" he glanced at Merry "—guests is ill."

He replaced the receiver and turned back to

her, cautiously relieving the pressure on her chest as he sat upon the desk beside her, blocking any chance of escape with his frame. He folded his hands on his knee and relaxed, watching her conversationally, waiting.

And Merry had to say it. "You followed me here, didn't you?" She was surprised at how even her voice was, how readily her mind was accepting and absorbing shock after shock. She should have been screaming. She should have been fighting and running and denying the constant, twisting betrayal at every turn. But she could speak. She could think. Survival instinct, she supposed.

Roger nodded benevolently. "I spend a lot of time out here."

"That's why Kevin didn't remember seeing you," she realized out loud. "Because you never tried to see him. You told us you did, but you didn't."

"Now, that's not strictly true," he objected. "I see Kevin—" He smiled. "Brother Light—quite a bit. I just didn't happen to see him that weekend. There was no point."

"How long?" she wanted to know, quietly, almost objectively.

Now his smile was indulgent. "More years than you want to count, dear." He tilted his head a little, not begrudging her a full explanation now that she was at his mercy—seeming, in fact, to enjoy explaining to her. "Actually, Abraham Samuels and I go back a long way. We were on the same debating team in college. We were two of a kind even then, which is why we became such great friends. Both of us had but a single ambition—to get ahead the quickest and easiest way possible." He chuckled. "He chose religion. I chose law. There's a strange compatibility there, if you think about it.

"Naturally," he continued, "when the organization started swinging big time, who should Abe call on for legal help but his old college buddy? And what should the old college buddy find when he got here but a veritable gold mine?" He shrugged. "It was expedient, of course, for me to stay 'undercover,' so to speak, to keep up my little law practice and a good standing in the community. I could work far more effecively that way. The Astra project," he boasted, "was my idea, and I've been mostly responsible for recruiting the talent it will take to see it through."

"And that's how Kevin got involved."

Roger nodded. "I don't generally get involved in bringing in the little sheep, as Abe calls them, but a certain quota is expected every now and then to keep up appearances. He was young, impressionable—a prime candidate."

And Merry looked at him levelly. "Why not me?"

He grinned. "Too damn stubborn. And too much trouble. You don't have what we like to call a malleable personality, and instability is one thing we don't need. We have to count on everything being under control."

"Why, Roger?" she asked flatly. "Why are you doing this?"

He glanced at the folder that now rested casually on the desk top. "I should think the answer would be obvious: money, power. And this is the grandest scheme ever devised by man. It's too close to completion now to risk any complications."

"Money," she parroted tonelessly. As Mark had said, "It all comes down to money."

He cocked his head in light concession. "A valuable lesson for you. The world is not ruled by the dreamers and the mystics but those who hold the purse strings. Facts and figures are what count, dear, not ideals."

Roger glanced around as Kevin came into the room. Only it wasn't Kevin, of course. It was Brother Light. He smiled at Meredith but showed no sign of recognition or surprise. If she had held any dim hope for help from her brother, it was gone. He was not, as far as Kevin was concerned, even her brother anymore. He was Brother Light, and he did as he was told.

"This young lady appears to be undergoing some distress." Roger informed him mildly. "Perhaps you could give her something to help her relax."

Kevin smiled and opened his bag. Merry watched him prepare the syringe. "What is it?" she asked conversationally. "Are you going to poison me?"

Roger chuckled. "No, no, nothing so inconvenient. Thorazine," he told her. "We use it sometimes on our more ... excitable children. It opens their minds and helps prepare them for the way of true enlightenment."

Merry did not take her eyes off the man who

once had been her brother. "That's what you did to Holly," she commented.

For a moment Roger looked confused. Then he remembered. "Oh, yes, the recruit you were seen talking to on your first visit." And he shook his head sadly. "Unfortunately, there is an occasional outbreak of worldliness even in our little utopia, and more effective methods are called for. Carefully supervised electroshock proves most effective—followed, of course, by maintenance dosages of Thorazine until our devotees are strong enough to carry on their missions alone."

They had it down to a science. Little wonder they had grown so strong. There was no room for error.

Kevin gently pushed up her sleeve and swabbed her arm with alcohol. "So what are you going to do with me?" she asked Roger.

"Keep you here awhile," he responded easily. "Perhaps you'll come to like it so much you'll never want to leave. There may be hope for you yet, Merry," he said smiling. He reached forward to touch her cheek. "I'm really sorry it didn't work out for us, dear," he said softly. "But perhaps now—"

Merry had always been stronger than her brother. Kevin, not programmed for violence, did not know how to respond. Roger was lazy and out of shape; he did not expect her to strike her brother. Like all of them, he had grown incautious in complacency.

She brought her feet up hard against the desk,

and the rollered chair shot across the light-piled carpet as the back of her arm crashed against Kevin's, sending him reeling backward. The chair toppled over, but she was out of it in a flash; she caught a blurred glimpse of Roger's face, his startled movement to rise, but she was faster than he was and at the door before he had taken a step.

In those flashing seconds she did not think about how far she would get; she did not think about the security of this prison; she did not think about the thousands of blank smiling faces waiting to capture her. She was running; she had reached the threshold; she was free.

And then strong arms grabbed her, cutting off her breath, whirling her around, and she looked straight into the face of Mark Brasfield.

Chapter Twelve

Meredith wanted to scream. Not because she was frightened but because it was too much. After having come so close and being betrayed at every turn, it was too much that in her final moment of escape it should be Mark who stopped her. Mark, whom she loved; Mark, whose first betrayal had been the most bitter; Mark, who was going to turn her over to these madmen.

She felt the horror and the pain and defeat rising like a tidal wave inside her, but no sound would come from her lips except the choked, gasping sounds of straining breath. She knew she should fight, she knew she should run, but her knees were weak. She couldn't make her legs move, and it seemed in that brief space of time as though Mark were supporting her, not restraining her.

Then other bodies crowded the doorway, pushing by with purpose and determination — blue uniforms, men in suits with badges — and the voice of one of them rose with quiet authority above the din of pattering incomprehension that was clamoring in her head: "Don't move, gentlemen. The compound has been sealed off, and I have a court order for search and seizure of your records, as well as the authority to detain all of you for questioning. Just remain calm, please."

There was movement and activity in the room and in the corridor behind them. Policemen standing warily near Roger and Kevin, ready to leap upon them if they tried to move. Men in suits turning keys in the locked file cabinets. It was all a blur to Merry, like a photograph taken from a fast-moving vehicle. She saw the dumb incomprehension on Kevin's face and the shock turn slowly to rage on Roger's, a darkening color and a murderous gaze that was directed toward Mark as he spat out, "You bastard."

Mark's voice was very cold. "Forget it, Blake," he said.

Mark's arms were still around Merry's ribs in a crushing hold, but his embrace seemed more sheltering than threatening, and her mind was darting back and forth, thoughts flinging themselves up against brick walls at every turn, bouncing back to her in pitiful wails of helpless confusion. She heard Mark's voice, dimly, and saw the distant blur of his face, gentled with concern, as he inquired, "Are you all right?"

The only sound that could escape her was a sob, and she shook her head, over and over again, in subconscious denial of what she could not understand and dared not hope for. Only one thing was clear: her mission still was not completed. She broke away from Mark as she saw a uniformed man roughly jerk Kevin's hands behind his back and snap cuffs on his wrists. "Don't hurt him!" she cried and ran to her brother.

Kevin did not struggle. He did not protest on his own behalf; he simply looked dazed and confused. The officer did not release his hold on Kevin, and she pleaded, "Let him go! He won't hurt anyone. He's—" The next was almost a sob. "He's my brother."

A momentary sympathy crossed the man's face. "I'm sorry, miss. I've got orders."

Mark came up behind her. His touch on her shoulder was gentle. "He'll have to be interrogated, Merry. When they find out he was nothing more than another victim, I'm sure you'll be able to take him home."

Meredith heard nothing but the word "home," and it steadied her, calmed her, filled her with hope. She touched Kevin's arm, softening her voice. She looked at him with eyes begging him to understand. "Did you hear that, Kevin? We can go home. It won't be much longer now. You're going home, and everything is going to be all right."

He looked at her slowly. Through the shock and disorientation in his eyes, she thought she saw a vague glimmer of understanding. "Home? But... I am home." He looked around the room, confusion mounting. "Where is Father Samuels? What—"

Through her choking disappointment and rising frustration, Merry felt again the gentle squeeze of Mark's hand on her shoulder. "It will take time," he assured her quietly. He spoke to Kevin. "Go with these men. They want to talk to you. And afterward, you're going home, with Merry."

Kevin looked at her again for a long time. Again, far beyond the heavy veils that shrouded his eyes, she thought she saw something flutter. And he said simply, hesitantly, as though testing the word, "Home." Then the officer led him away.

Meredith's eyes were burning, and her throat was tight. She could not speak or move for a long time. There was so much she still did not understand. Nothing made sense, but she held on to one small but certain truth: it was over. Somehow it was over, and she was going to take Kevin home. He would be all right; she would make sure of it. Everything would be all right.

Mark's arm slipped around her shoulders. He spoke quietly to one of the men in a business suit, then began to lead her away.

"We can't leave the compound," he was saying as he pushed open a door onto a small, quiet courtyard, "but we can sit out here until the furor dies down." She looked up at him helplessly, and he shook his head, his face grim. "No, don't try to talk yet. You need some air. Just sit here and relax."

He pushed her gently down onto a low stone bench, and he did not take his arm from around her shoulders. Merry was glad.

The day was gray and cool with the threat of rain, the air gentle and fragrant. Images kept flashing through her head. Roger, so calm and confident. Kevin, coming toward her with that syringe. Mark, catching her in his arms. But they were distant images, a long-ago memory. Later, the shock would overtake her. Later, the emotional trauma would nearly rip her apart. Now it was all she could do to try to understand it.

She took slow, steady breaths, trying to force life into the numbed cells of her brain. Mark took her cold hands in both of his and began to rub them lightly, warming them. Eventually, she could think again. And, understanding, Mark began to answer her questions before she even asked them.

"I didn't know anything about this, Merry," he said quietly. "Not until I saw those notes you had the other night. Even then I couldn't believe what they implied, which is probably one reason I blew up at you so crazily." His lips curved into a smile that was only an imitation of his old cynical quirk. "It was a very clever operation," he said. "Not one of the men in the finance department had the whole picture; each of us just had a different piece of it. Only Samuels and top managers like Roger knew what was really going on. That way they could be sure there was no leak." And he sighed. "Oh, I knew there were some slightly shady dealings coming down, but I figured it was par for the course, and I never wanted to get involved." He looked at her. "Until you."

He shifted his eyes away, gazing solemnly at the dusty-winged butterfly that hovered over a nearby tulip. "Those notes—your theories—kept haunting me, and yesterday I started making some phone calls. Last night, after you left, I came back here and started putting things together. This morning I pulled some strings and got a fast court order." Again the slight lift of his lips was strained, and he looked at her. "The federal government," he told her, "doesn't take too kindly to private organizations manipulating the economy on a global scale."

Gradually, it came together for Merry. Mark. He wasn't behind it, after all. He was an innocent victim, as she was. He was on her side. He had succeeded where she had failed. "I'm—I thought," she said somewhat hoarsely, "you didn't care."

Her anxiously searching eyes saw his face soften helplessly, almost as though with surprise at his own actions. "I didn't," he said simply. He released a breath and entwined his fingers with hers, dropping his eyes to study them. "For what it's worth," he said, "you came along and in less than a week changed living patterns and thinking habits it took a lifetime of bitterness to form. You turned my values upside down. You started me thinking about things like involvement and integrity and principles. Commitment."

He met her eyes briefly, hesitantly. "I've made some mistakes, Merry," he said. "Bad ones. And for the first time in my life I'm ashamed of them. I know you can't forgive me for deceiving you in the first place, but it may help you to know that I don't forgive myself, either, and that because of it, I've changed."

Merry looked at him, still having difficulty accepting it, understanding it. Her eyes searched his face, probed inside his mind, and there were no barriers there now; all she saw was the truth. "It wasn't you." She had to say it out loud. "It wasn't you who ordered Brother Chi—"

Again Mark shook his head, and this time his smile seemed more natural. "Dennis," he corrected. "His name is Dennis Fuller. And no one ordered him to do anything. That's another thing I found out last night. He's not a part of any of this. He's a professional deprogrammer, and he came for Holly. He saw you with me and naturally assumed you were trouble. Then, after Holly talked to you and—" He dropped his eyes in remembrance of Holly's fate. "Naturally, he thought you were responsible. These guys can be pretty rough. They have to be," he finished bleakly.

A stab of pain, the first she had felt acutely since entering the building that morning, plucked at her as she thought of Holly...and of Kevin, so innocent, so confused, so completely lost in the upheaval of his world. "What will happen to them?" she whispered. "What will happen to Holly, to Kevin...?"

"They've got a hard road ahead of them," Mark replied grimly. "Some of them will be reoriented into mainstream society; others will drift back into places like this. There's no guarantee which will be which." And then he smiled at her. "But I think Kevin, with a sister like you on his side, has a better chance than most."

Merry thought so, too. For the first time in her

life she was sure enough of herself to know what she could do—for Kevin, for her parents, for herself. She could promise them all a future.

But then she looked at Mark anxiously. "And Samuels?"

"If he's not in custody by now, he will be shortly," replied Mark. "I don't think there's much chance we'll have to worry about him again for a while."

They looked at each other in a moment that was too full and too poignant for words. There were questions and uncertainties, hopes and fears, drawing them closer and pushing them apart, all of it too intense to be dealt with at once, in this moment. Then Mark's eyes moved uncomfortably away. He said, "I guess we'd better go back in, if you're strong enough. The investigators will want to talk to you."

But he did not release her hand. For another moment he looked straight ahead, seeming undecided. And then he turned back to her. His face was tight with emotion he did not want to force on her, but his eyes filled with all the things he did not feel free to say. "Merry," he began uncertainly, "I just wanted to say . . ." Then his hand came up to lightly stroke her cheek. "Thank you for coming into my life."

Merry closed her eyes, and her arms came up slowly, instinctively, to circle him. She brought her face against his chest, the emotions that flooded her too powerful to be analyzed, too simple to be denied. "All I ever wanted," she said brokenly, "was to love you."

She heard his swift intake of breath, felt the cautious tightening of his arms, then the desperation in his muscles, as he pulled her closer, and closer. His lips were against her hair and then upon her face, touching her lips with wondrous question. And the kiss that blossomed and grew between them answered all questions, banished all shadows, sealed the bond that had undergone so much battering but still survived intact. They each had made mistakes; neither was perfect. But together they could find their way.

Merry's head was against his shoulder; she could feel the thumping of his heart intermingling with her own. Though there was no sun, warmth was spilling over her and light was growing from inside. Contentment. This was what it felt like. She had known it all along.

Mark's hand was a little unsteady as he stroked her hair. In a moment he lifted his face. "You know, don't you," he inquired soberly, his voice not quite even, "that I'll probably be implicated in this thing?"

Merry looked at him calmly, lovingly. "You'll plea-bargain for turning state's evidence," she promised him. "You won't be charged."

A slight anxiety crossed his eyes. "Do you think so?"

Merry smiled. "If you can wait a couple of years for a certain 'almost-lawyer' to get her license, I can guarantee it."

And she saw the worry and the uncertainty on his face fade into quiet joy; his eyes were deep with it. "If the lawyer is as stubborn and idealistic as you are," he replied, "it will be worth the wait."

And then his expression changed. He cupped her face with his hands and looked into her eyes intensely. "Merry," he said hoarsely, "I know I have a lot of faults. I may never be the man that you want me to be. But if you'll let me love you, I'll try."

Merry wrapped her arms around him, pressing herself against him, and that was all the answer he needed. His arms enfolded her tightly, and they stayed that way for a long time, holding each other.

EYE OF THE STORM

MAURA SEGER

A powerful
portrayal of
the events of
World War II in the
Pacific, *Eye of the Storm* is a riveting story of how love
triumphs over hatred. In this, the first of a three-book
chronicle, Army nurse Maggie Lawrence meets Marine
Sgt. Anthony Gargano. Despite military regulations
against fraternization, they resolve to face together
whatever lies ahead.... Author Maura Seger, also known
to her fans as Laurel Winslow, Sara Jennings, Anne
MacNeil and Jenny Bates, was named 1984's
Most Versatile Romance Author by *The Romantic Times*.

Share the joys and sorrows of real-life love with
Harlequin American Romance!™·

GET THIS BOOK FREE as your introduction to Harlequin American Romance — an exciting series of romance novels written especially for the American woman of today.

Mail to:
Harlequin Reader Service

In the U.S.
2504 West Southern Ave.
Tempe, AZ 85282

In Canada
P.O. Box 2800, Postal Station A
5170 Yonge St., Willowdale, Ont. M2N 5T5

YES! I want to be one of the first to discover
Harlequin American Romance. Send me FREE and without obligation *Twice in a Lifetime.* If you do not hear from me after I have examined my FREE book, please send me the 4 new **Harlequin American Romances** each month as soon as they come off the presses. I understand that I will be billed only $2.25 for each book (total $9.00). There are no shipping or handling charges. There is no minimum number of books that I have to purchase. In fact, I may cancel this arrangement at any time. *Twice in a Lifetime* is mine to keep as a FREE gift, even if I do not buy any additional books.

154-BPA-NAZJ

Name	(please print)

Address	Apt. no.

City	State/Prov.	Zip/Postal Code

Signature (If under 18, parent or guardian must sign.)

AMR-SUB-1